Strong Side

An Eastshore Tigers Novel

Alison Hendricks

AUGUST

CHAPTER ONE
- Derek -

Putting on that blue and black jersey for the first time feels like coming home.

Sure, it's just a flimsy mesh shirt that barely stretches over my pads. But to me, it represents a hell of a lot more: A long road full of struggle, and a way to move on with my life.

Mostly, it feels fucking amazing to get the chance to play football again.

As a recruited walk-on, I was offered the chance to attend the Tigers' summer camp. While it's technically voluntary, it's pretty much expected for anyone who wants to start this season.

Honestly, I probably would've gone even if it wasn't mandatory. Lifting weights for hours a day and running sprints in the sweltering Florida heat isn't exactly my idea of fun, but it's helped me get my head back into the game. And it's given me a chance to meet some of my teammates. Considering I've been at Eastshore College for two years already and can only really count my roommates among my friends, it's probably a good thing.

But summer camp and fall practice are two totally different beasts. This is the first time we're all together on the same field, and it'll be the first time we run actual plays. Of course, that doesn't mean there aren't conditioning drills hammered into us from day one.

Weighed down by my practice equipment, I'm put through my paces with the most grueling drills imaginable. Up-downs that lead into bear crawls that lead right into suicides.

It's fucking brutal, and if I hadn't experienced something similar in high school, I'd probably be puking my guts out right now. As it is, I've seen at least four guys run off the field and start retching. Either they're not used to this level of heat and humidity, or the hard work required of them. Maybe it's a combination of the two.

Either way, they're probably not going to make it to the first game. That's why coaches do these drills right at the start—to send the weaker guys home. There's nothing even remotely relaxing about college football, and I knew that going into it.

It's not like my thighs aren't jelly by the time we're done, or that my chest doesn't burn from trying to wheeze in a few extra breaths during sprints. But compared to what I've gone through in the past, it's almost a privilege to be able to do all this shit.

And it honestly could be worse. The NCAA regulates the first few practices of the season, so Coach Garvey blows the whistle on us at regular intervals, switching out groups of guys and letting the rest of us take a much-needed break.

Some of the guys almost collapse, and I

don't really blame them. Just an hour and a half into it, and I'm completely drenched in sweat. My pads are sticking to my shirt, and that's practically plastered to my body. Even still, there's a flood of endorphins running through my veins right now as I jog over to the sidelines, desperate for a drink of water.

I find the tepid cooler and pour myself a cup, unsure where I left my actual bottle. One gulp downs it, and I fill up a few more times before I have competition.

"And I thought my coach was a hard-ass," a familiar voice says.

I look up to see Troy Sanders, a freshman walk-on, recruited the same way I was. Troy is one of the first guys I talked to here.

"Guess Garvey didn't get his rep from letting his team slack off," he continues. "I'm gonna end up icing my shoulder by the end of this, I know it."

"You won't be the only one."

I have a feeling the locker room is already stocked with a freezer full of ice packs to handle the demand. And probably a supply cabinet's worth of athletic tape, too. It's always rough like this over the first few weeks. It has to be.

I clap Sanders on the back, his pads rattling underneath his practice jersey. None of us have names out here. Just numbers that have been used again and again. For the guys who don't start, this is all they'll get for the entire season.

Guys like Sanders will get to stay at Eastshore whether he starts in every game or not.

The chances of me earning funding for the rest of my time here are pretty fucking slim, but they'll be absolutely demolished if I never play a game.

"You looked good out there during pass drills, man."

His compliment makes me feel like an asshole, but I guess that's the world of college football.

"You did, too. Could tell when your shoulder started giving you trouble, though."

Sanders lets out a sigh, dragging his hand over his face. He swallows down a gulp of water, then finally responds. "Fuck. You think anybody else noticed?"

"Half the guys out here are nursing a strain. I wouldn't worry about it."

He looks out at the field, and I follow his gaze to a bigger linebacker who's trying to cover up a limp. Probably got his ankle fucked up during suicides.

"Yeah, you're probably right."

Sanders and I fall quiet, and the only sound is the suffering of our teammates until a loud, feminine whistle from the bleachers draws our attention. A group of three women are on their feet, one of them holding up a sign that says "I Love Hawk," with a picture of a hawk instead of the word. I think there's a phone number at the bottom, too.

"Should've just written 'I love cock'," Sanders says.

"Don't be an asshole." I punch his shoulder, but I doubt he even feels it through the pads.

"Hey, I speak from a place of jealousy, trust me. You know that guy probably gets more pussy than everybody on this team combined. And *his* shoulder's probably loose as—"

"Don't even finish that."

My gaze moves to the object of their admiration. Jason "Hawk" Hawkins is an All-Star senior. I'm pretty sure he would've been a Heisman winner last year, if the Tigers had placed a little bit better.

I've never officially met the guy, but it's impossible to play for the Tigers—and even attend Eastshore College—without knowing who he is, if only by reputation. I don't know how much of what they say is true, but he's definitely the golden boy of ESC.

As I watch him in the middle of his passing drills, I can see why. His form is fucking flawless. Ball after ball, he just drops right back and fires off a shot. Every one of them connects, and I'm not sure if it's just because he's that talented, or because he has enough confidence to force the ball to behave the way he wants it to.

He could be a total prick, and it would still be hard not to admire him. He's indisputably the best player on campus, and probably better than Eastshore deserves. His influence on the school will have a lasting effect; he's the reason the Tigers have been able to make a name for themselves in Division-I football.

And from everything I've heard, Hawk actually isn't a prick. Sure, he's a little... distant. He seems like the type of guy who thinks about football nonstop. But it's hard not to wonder what it would be like to get to know him; to bask in his dedication.

I know how that sounds, but some athletes just bring everybody else up with them.

And it doesn't hurt that he's sexy as hell.

The first time I saw him take off his helmet, I was watching an ESC game in my dorm room. It's probably a good thing my roommates weren't around, because I spent a full five minutes just staring at the TV, rewinding the DVR.

Sanders may be jealous of Hawk for getting more pussy than anybody else on the team, but there's a part of me that sympathizes with those girls in the stands. My sexuality isn't something I intend to broadcast to my teammates, but if I hadn't known I was gay before this, Hawk is the type of guy who would've definitely made me question myself.

As it stands, I've pretty much done everything in my power to avoid him so far, just to keep from looking like a complete idiot. Even if Hawk and I to play for the same team—and it seems really fucking unlikely—he's way out of my league.

"—But I tell you what, man. You get in with Hawk, and you've got it made. No way you wouldn't start."

Shit. Sanders has been talking this whole time. I'm glad he's got a little bit of a narcissistic streak, otherwise he probably would've called me out on staring at one of our teammates and admiring the way his tight ass flexes when he throws the ball.

Fuck. So much for not acting gay around the team, but it's hard not to think about a guy like Hawk that way. He's the poster boy for confidence and raw masculinity.

"So you're saying, what? Find out his favorite type of bran cereal and bribe the shit out of him?"

Or give him a full body massage. Though that would probably benefit me more than him.

Thankfully Sanders laughs at my suggestion. At least I haven't managed to make it noticeably weird on the first day of practice.

"Hey man, whatever you gotta do. Guy's gotta stay regular. Don't think I won't steal that idea, though."

"Every receiver for himself," I agree.

Before I can chug another cup full of water, Coach Garvey blows the whistle on the other guys, signaling us to endure more punishment.

But as I start to take the field, I see Coach walk out to the 50 yard line where he can be heard by most of us.

"All right, we've got a couple hours left, so here's what we're going to do. If you've got a black patch in your jersey, you're running scrimmage. Offense and defense. Two teams. Everybody else, you're running 40s until the next whistle."

The other coaches repeat what Garvey said, and I can hear Sanders cuss up a storm beside me. "Trade you jerseys."

"Yeah, I'll pass. Don't bitch too much. I'll be right where you are pretty soon."

"Not soon enough. "He grins at me, though. And claps me on the shoulder pad. "Go make daddy proud."

I have no idea if he's talking about Garvey, Hawk, or himself. But as soon as I look downfield, I see Hawk gathering with a bunch of other guys. And all of them have black patches on their jerseys.

This is my shot. Either I'll impress him, or make a complete ass of myself.

I figure there's about a 50/50 chance either way.

CHAPTER TWO
- Jason -

Feeling the laces beneath my fingers is like finally being able to breathe again; coming up for air after spending so long nearly drowning.

Yeah, maybe it's a little dramatic. But between academics, family, and relationships, I feel like the rest of my life is just some massive cinderblock tied to my ankle, not giving a single fuck as I sink to the bottom.

But football carries me up to the surface. It always has. No matter what's been going on in my life, as soon as I pick up that ball, I'm me again. Not Jason Hawkins, the senior who probably isn't going to graduate. But Hawk, the cool, confident quarterback who knows how to get a ball down the field time and time again.

Out here, I'm in my element. I know there are a couple reporters in the stands, and maybe a recruiter or two from the NFL, but it doesn't faze me. If they're here for me, great. My dad would probably tell me I need to hustle my ass off just in case.

But if I think about that, I'm going to choke for sure. So instead, I assume they're here for somebody else.

As I jog up to the huddle, joining guys I never really feel bonded with until we're all in uniform, I focus on what I need to do. A quarterback's success is determined by how he reacts under pressure, and even if it's taken me a long time to get to where I am today, I'm determined to be the guy this team needs.

After all, this is my last chance. Even if I don't graduate, I won't be eligible to play next year. I've done my five seasons. Gotten as much out of my college career as I possibly can. Now it's on me to bring it home and get the Tigers their first ever Division-I bowl game win.

And it's gonna happen one step at a time.

Coach Garvey runs down a short list of plays he wants to make sure we work in. Most of the starters already know them by heart, so this is probably for the walk-ons and rookies. I'd say 3/4 of the scrimmage team is made up of guys who already know the drill. It's a good mix, and it'll give Coach a chance to see what the new guys can do.

As far as I'm concerned, it's a chance to find that one guy I can count on. The receiver or running back—or hell, even the tight end—who's going to help me do what needs to be done. Somebody who's focused and committed and willing to take this seriously.

I love my teammates. They're like the brothers I never had, as stupid as it sounds. But most of them aren't here with hopes of continuing on to the NFL, and I need somebody who's willing to take it all the way.

The coaches head back to the sidelines to watch, with Assistant Coach Hanes supervising the guys still running drills. I call the first play, taking a pretty standard formation out of our playbook, then jog up to the line of scrimmage.

Getting my hands on the ball again gets my

blood pumping. Practice may not be a real game, but it makes my brain light up like a fucking fireworks show. As soon as my fingers touch those laces, I'm in the zone.

I drop back, trusting the line to hold, and scan for the receiver who's supposed to be cutting across the field. I see Matthews making the route, but he's slower than he should be.

I give him the benefit of the doubt, hoping he'll put on a burst of speed. I let the ball fly while I still have a straight shot without any interference. But just as I guessed, Matthews isn't in position for the catch. The ball bounces off the tips of his gloves, and then off the tips of a cornerback's gloves, before it hits the ground.

It bugs the shit out of me when guys aren't doing what they're supposed to do, especially when I know they're more than capable. But Coach has already gotten on my case before about trying to do his job for him, and I keep my mouth shut, just giving Matthews a "what the fuck, man" look when he takes his place at the line.

Second and ten is hardly the worst odds I've ever faced, though. Calling out the play, I look to my left and see one of our new receivers. I usually keep tabs on the guys who come in for offense, and this year is no different.

Derek Griffin, walk-on junior. I don't know much about him beyond that. But when I see him standing loose and ready to run, I give him the nod. His helmet tilts down as he nods back, and I take the snap.

The center is off-balance, leaning too much

on his left side. He sprained his right ankle over the summer, and now he's favoring it. But that means the snap is a little off-balance.

It takes me a minute to adjust, and by the time I do, all hell breaks loose. The defense is taking advantage of my line's weaknessh. One of the leaner guys, Jeffries, breaks away from the tackle, pivots, and starts toward me.

I don't have time to set up the way I want. I just have to find an open guy, fling the ball, and hope for the best. I hate doing it this way, but it's an unavoidable part of football.

By the time I get rid of the ball, I've only got one foot planted. There's no hope for a tight spiral, and I watch as it sails languidly toward Griffin.

There's no way I can be pissed at him if he doesn't make the play. It's a hard catch for even the experienced guys to make. But I can see in his posture that he's making the calculations in his head. Deciding how much he's going to have to compensate to catch that ball.

He cuts past a defender, and manages an underhanded catch to grab hold of the ball before it hits the ground. Tucking it close to his body, he runs for the sidelines, and we get a surprisingly easy first down.

I jog up to meet the new position, and clap Griffin on the arm. "Good catch."

He doesn't say anything for a moment, but I can see him smile behind his facemask. He's got a pretty nice smile for a football player. Then again, we're never as bad off as the hockey guys.

"Thanks."

"You ready for another?"

He nods, taking the position. His fingers skim the grass, and I call the next play. He's off like a shot, beating the defender who seems to half-ass it. It's Matthews they cover, thinking I'll probably favor him.

I take advantage of their mistake, and deliberately overthrow to Griffin. Either he knew what I meant by "another", or he's just that good at reading where the ball will end up, because he compensates for it easily, putting on a burst of speed and plucking the ball from the air.

By the time anybody catches up to him, we've gained another 30 yards.

Griffin and I keep it up, and is not long before we score a touchdown. He seems to be able to catch every shitty thing I throw at him, and it's almost like he can read exactly what I'm going to do before I do it. I have this weird feeling—almost a sort of giddiness—that this is the guy who's going to make it happen for me. This is the guy I can count on.

I can't help but notice the fact that he always seems eager to step the ball out of bounds, though. Maybe he was just taught to do it that way. A lot of high school coaches prefer stopping the clock every chance they get, and avoiding injury whenever possible for their star players. Still, some gut feeling tells me to keep an eye on it.

The second team's offense takes the field, and we hit the sidelines. I watch special teams set up, but I can see Matthews out of the corner of my eye. He's heading straight for me, and he's stomping around like an enraged bull.

The helmet comes off, the mouthguard is spit out, and he gets right up in my face. I can feel my body tense, and I take a step back to put some distance between us.

"What the fuck was that?"

"You have to be a little more specific," I say dryly, feeling a little bit of satisfaction when his face turns even redder.

Matthews is a pretty good athlete, but he's always been kind of a tool. And while I can't prove it, I'm pretty sure he's been getting into some serious PED use.

"Don't fucking play with me, Hawk. I was wide open, and you throw it to this cocksucker?"

"You were covered by two guys on almost every play, Matthews."

I can see Griffin nearby, and the corner of my mouth turns up in what I hope is an apologetic expression.

"And I still could've caught the ball."

"Sure didn't look that way," I say, knowing I'm tempting fate.

"What the fuck did you say to me?"

"Knock it off, Matthews," I hear Garvey bark a little further down the sidelines.

Nobody's surprised by Matthews' willingness to pick a fight. He's always been like this, and it's only gotten worse in the last year or two. If he wasn't a damn good receiver, I think Coach would've probably canned him after his first season.

"Fine. You wanna piss our season away, go

right ahead."

Fucking dramatic, too.

He storms off, grabs a water bottle, and chugs it like he's downing a bottle of Jack.

"Nice to have an arch-enemy on the first day of practice," Griffin says as Matthews passes him, giving him what I can only assume is a death glare.

A grin comes easy to me for the first time today. Once football season nears, I'm usually all business. It's nice to loosen up a little.

Griffin walks up to me and finally takes his helmet off. His brown hair is matted down by sweat, and he has the typical, slightly flushed look of an athlete who's just worked his ass off.

"Thanks for that," he says.

I shrug. "No thanks needed. You made yourself open, so I gave you the ball."

Something glints in his green eyes, and the corner of his mouth turns up in a smile.

"I passed the test, then?"

I grin back at him. "Yeah, you did."

The second team can't make it down the field. They have to give it up after an unsuccessful attempt to convert a fourth down, and we take the field again.

For the rest of practice, I'm determined to improve my own performance. My thoughts turn inward, and I block out everything but my form as I handle the ball, and the guys I need to get it to to put more points on the board. It's just a practice, but every game, every scrimmage is a chance for improvement. I have to look at it that way, or I'm never going to get us to a bowl game. And I'm definitely never going to get picked up by the NFL.

I spread the love around during this drive, letting my backs run the ball, handing off to Matthews and to Harding as well as Griffin. We don't get the score, but it's not long before we take the field again.

I know Coach is probably going to call time on us after this drive, and I want to put in the best show possible. The defense has really tightened up, falling back into the groove of reading our patterns.

Third and eight, I drop back and look for a receiver. The defense has been all over my ass this time, and covering my runner step for step. They know I have to throw it, and they've got guys covering Matthews and Griffin.

Matthews is probably the safe bet. He has more experience dealing with a tight defense, and after what happened earlier, he'll probably work extra hard just to make sure he doesn't look bad.

But I want to see if I can get it to Griffin. He's being chased down by two guys, with a blocker only able to take care of one of them. He tries to cut across and lose one, and I can see him look back to me, ready for the pass.

I snap off a straight shot, following through even as a linebacker comes within feet of tackling me. My focus isn't on him, but on Griffin.

The defender manages to shake his blocker, and there are two guys heading straight for Griffin now. It's a shitty situation for any receiver, and I curse myself for not going with Matthews.

I expect the ball to be batted away, but it's worse than that. Griffin just chokes completely. He cuts the route short, ducking the defenders, and one picks it off like I'd intentionally thrown it to him.

He makes it a good twenty yards before he's brought down, and I can't help but wonder if this is a sign of my dreams going up in smoke already.

CHAPTER THREE
- Derek -

I thought I was over this. I thought I was better.

But as soon as I'm faced with a tackle, I just freeze. My muscles lock up, my brain screams at me to get the fuck out of the way, and I can't seem to override it. Seeing those two guys rushing toward me, it's just a straight shot of bad memories.

It all happens in a flash. I remember the pain; a sharp ache coursing down my spine and into my legs. And then nothing at all.

This time, at least I can feel *something*. I feel the defender bump into me as he tries to slow his momentum. I feel the rush of air as his teammate snatches the ball and runs it down the field. I can't seem to make myself move to stop him, so I just stand there and watch uselessly as he's finally run out of bounds.

There's a reason I avoided playing football for the first couple of years at Eastshore. I thought it was over it, but it's like it's happening all over again.

I can hear my teammates swearing and yelling, and the harsh whistle from Coach Garvey as he calls us back to the sidelines. Someone herds me over there, and somehow I get my feet to work.

Some of the guys talk shit under their breath, and they have every right. What good is a football player who's afraid of getting tackled?

"Griffin," I hear Coach say, and his voice is

rough with disappointment. "Come over here minute."

The walk of shame has never felt more real. At least this time I know they're talking about my performance, not my personal life.

Coach Garvey waits patiently at the end of the line, and I can see Hawk standing beside him. Great. That's exactly what I need.

Sanders said the way to a starting position was getting in good with Hawk. It seems like I'm going to find out if the inverse is true now.

"What happened out there, son?"

The day I signed my papers, Coach Garvey asked me about my high school career. And about the day that ended it. I told him the truth back then, and I know that's why he's not just tearing into me.

I almost wish he didn't know, though. I'm pretty sure he would rip into any other guy who did what I did.

"I don't know. I froze up. It won't happen again, Coach."

"You know I don't have any use for a football player who's afraid of getting tackled, Griffin. I told you that when I brought you on."

"I know," I say, in a voice that sounds small to me.

"I can work with him, Coach."

Coach and I are both surprised by Hawk's sudden interest.

"You know that's not going to guarantee you the captain spot, Hawkins. Anything you choose to do with Griffin has to be on your own

24

time."

"He's a good receiver. Shows a lot of potential. I think he can get over this. Right?" He finishes, looking at me.

I'm too shocked to speak. Hell, shocked doesn't even begin to cover it. Hawk doesn't know me. Even the completions I pulled off today don't stack up against that massive fail.

But for some reason, he wants to help me.

"Jesus," I hear the other receiver grumble. "What did you do, rookie? Suck him off before practice?"

I'm still too stunned by Hawk's offer to react. I'm used to this kind of locker room talk; there's no way I could play any kind of sport without having a thick skin. But there's still a small part of me that wonders if he knows.

Right now, though, it's the least of my worries.

I never told Coach Garvey I was gay, but I think he knew, regardless. I'm glad he didn't encourage me to tell the other guys.

It would only bring out the worst in everybody involved. At least this time, I know Matthews is just saying it because he's an asshole. Not because he thinks it might be true.

"Thank you for volunteering to start your 40s right now, Matthews," Coach says.

For a second, it looks like Matthews is going to stand up to him. But even he's not that stupid, apparently. He tosses his helmet and jogs off toward where the other guys are running their drills.

"Hawkins, if you want to take on Griffin as your personal project, you have my blessing. You're right. He is a good player."

He claps me on the shoulder, then goes back to observing the teams on the field, leaving me staring up at Hawk. I'm a tall guy, but he has a couple inches on me. I'd say he's 6'3" or 6'4" at the least. A wall of solid muscle standing in front of me, scrutinizing my reaction.

I still can't believe he'd stick his neck out for me, and I really don't know what to say.

"Thanks," I manage, even though I owe him a lot more than that.

"Don't worry about it. Meet me after practice. We'll figure out a plan."

Just like that, he heads off to do his drills. I bust ass for the rest of practice, knowing I have a lot to make up for. But the whole time, I can't help but watch my new mentor. Having one-on-one time with Jason Hawkins is either going to cure me of every mental hangup, or give me another one entirely:

Him.

CHAPTER FOUR
- Jason -

As the shower comes to life and the water hits my chest, I inhale a deep breath of steam and let it clear my head.

The warmth soothes my aching muscles, and I hold back a groan of pleasure. Not really the kind of thing I want to share with my teammates. This is my time. There's an unspoken code here, and every guy knows not to talk in the shower. Unlike in the locker room, I don't have to expect somebody to come up to me and interrupt my thoughts.

I'm fair game in the locker room. Guys interrupt me mid-thought there. But here, I can play back the day in my mind and pick apart every detail.

Coach Garvey says I obsess over every tiny thing. I always figured a college coach would like that, but maybe I am a little intense about it. I can't really help it. This is all I know. It's the only thing I know how to do, and the only thing I'm good at.

If I don't put my all into improving, then I'm not working hard enough.

At least, that's what my dad always says. From the time he coached my peewee team, through my high school career, and now even in college, he's informed a lot of my views and behaviors when it comes football. I know what the outside observer would say: he's just a washed up old athlete who's pressuring his son to finish what he started.

But football is the only thing that really brings us together. So if he's pushing me to accomplish something he couldn't, I guess I feel like I have to give it all I've got.

For the first practice of the season, today wasn't too bad. A lot of the guys are sluggish, but right now, I'm focused on my own performance. Coach Garvey made it pretty clear my freshman year that if I tried to do his job for him, he'd throw me on the bench faster than I could blink. And after years of getting agitated by the guys who don't take it seriously—the guys who would rather get fucked up every night—I'm over it.

There are definitely a few things I'd change from today. I might have thrown poorly to Griffin on purpose, but there were a few plays where I could've set up better. A few situations where I could've made something out of nothing. I run them back in my head and try to think of the outcomes if I would've carried the ball instead of passing it. Or if I would've put a little more spin on it, or tried for a higher arc.

I'm still thinking about it as I head to my locker and grab my gym bag. I pull out my change of clothes and start ranking my performance for the day. It's something my dad always does, and I guess it just sort of carried over to me. Today, I give myself maybe a 4/5 for endurance, a 3.5/5 for accuracy, a 4/5 for speed, and a 3/5 for consistency.

It bugs me that I don't have an even spread across the board, but I don't have much of a chance to work out a plan before I'm interrupted.

"Looking good out there, Hawk. Guess you didn't take the summer off like the rest of us." Dante Mills and I have been friends since freshman year, when we roomed together in the Thompson Building. He knows how to push my buttons.

"Have to keep on top of it. We can't all be naturally gifted like you."

Mills grins, leaning against the locker beside mine. "True. You mortals have to work for a godlike body like this," he says, patting his stomach.

Dante is a big guy. He was probably 6 feet tall and at least 300 pounds in the seventh grade. It's all solid muscle, though, and as much as I'd kill for the kind of strength he has, I'm pretty thankful for my lean frame. Quarterbacks aren't built to be trucks. But offensive tackles are.

And Mills is the one lineman who's always had my back. Last year, he completely steamrolled a guy who took a sack after I'd already gotten rid of the ball. Both of them were ejected, but Mills was slapped with a three-game probation, too. After the game, he just gave me one of his trademark shit-eating grins, shrugged, and said it was worth it.

"Hey, I heard about your little pet project." He lowers his voice, and I turn to him with one brow raised.

"That supposed to be some kind of secret?"

"I guess not if you don't want it to be." He shrugs. "Just haven't seen you take on anybody but a QB before. You trying to get in good with Garvey for that captain's patch?"

In football, team captains don't mean as much as they do in other sports. It's still a badge of honor, though. Something I can put on a resume, and something the NFL will definitely notice.

"Figure it can't hurt. And if we're going to take it all the way this year, then every guy out there has to be at the top of his game."

"You really think he can start? Shit, with the way Matthews was looking at him earlier, I wouldn't be surprised if he ends up in traction."

I search the locker room, finding Matthews easily. He's still wearing a scowl, and pulling his clothes on like a two-year-old having a temper tantrum. Fucking A. Part of me wants to let Coach know there could be trouble, but I don't want to be *that guy.*

"Yeah, I think he's got a shot. He's as good as any of the starters from last year." Or better. But saying that in the middle of the locker room is just begging for trouble. "He caught every shit pass I threw him."

"Yeah, until he didn't. You can't count on a receiver who's pissing his pants every time somebody gets near him."

Mills leans back against the locker, folding his arms over his chest. He puts on his best analytical face, and in between pulling on my shirt and then my boxers, I watch him scan the room.

"Just don't hit it too hard, okay?"

The little edge of humor that always accompanies his words is gone. He staring at me, and for once his expression looks gravely serious. "Okay...?"

"I mean it. I know how you get, Hawk. You spend enough time on yourself. Just make sure you aren't putting too much into this guy. For his sake and yours."

I guess I should take it as a compliment. I never do things halfway. But he's right. There's already a really good chance I won't graduate this year. I've almost guaranteed it, taking the absolute minimum class load to make sure I have enough time to dedicate to football. Taking on another project pretty much ensures I'm going to need to cut some corners as far as school is concerned.

I don't feel great about it, but I didn't come to Eastshore for the education. I came to play football.

"Don't worry about it. I'll figure it out."

I tug on my jeans and grab my bag before closing my locker. Mills meets my gaze one last time, shrugs, then wanders back to his own spot. I find Griffin in the crowd and head toward him, slinging my bag over one shoulder.

"Meet me in the parking lot when you're ready."

"Just give me a sec and I'll be right out."

He's half dressed when he says it, wearing jeans but no shirt. He's a lot more cut than I would've expected for a receiver. Most of them are built for speed, lean and able to run as soon as they have the ball. But it's clear Griffin has put a lot of work into his body. His arms are built up, especially, and I feel a weird sort of flush pass through me as I look at him.

Damn, I've been here too long. I loaded up on carbs during breakfast, but after the intense workout, I'm starving again. That must be what it is.

Putting that weird sensation behind me, I head out into the parking lot near the stadium. During the off-season, it's easy for players to get a spot nearby. My blue Accord is parked between a beat up old Volvo and a hatchback that's missing two hubcaps. Not that my ride is in much better shape. I take care of her, but she's nothing fancy. Mostly just a way to get from point A to point B.

As I survey some of the other cars in the lot —especially the ones that look brand-new, waxed and just begging for rain—I wonder if my teammates just come from loaded families, or if they're blatantly breaking the NCAA's rule to not accept handouts from recruiters. I guess it's none of my business either way.

It only takes a few minutes for Griffin to get out here, and he jogs until he spots me. A tiny smile tugs up the corner of my lips. It's nice to see somebody with so much enthusiasm. I know the freshmen and new walk-ons sometimes grate on the veteran players, but to me, the rookies are the guys I usually connect with most. They know they have to make a name for themselves, so they're completely focused and committed.

"Got a car?"

"Nah, I took the bus."

I hit the button on the key fob and hear the click of the lock as it slides out of place on all four doors. "Come on. I'll give you a ride. You can put your stuff in the back."

I slide into the driver's seat and turn the key in the ignition. A Kansas song blares over the radio, and I reach for the volume button to turn it down.

"So," he says as he ducks into the seat beside me. "Should I call somebody and give them your description? Just in case they find the body later."

I can hear the nervous edge to his voice, and when I look over at him, he's smiling. I just laugh. "Don't bother. I'm a professional. They'll never find the body."

"Good to know. Where you kidnapping me to, then?"

"There's a sports bar downtown that a lot of the guys hit up after games. I figure we can work out a plan there. You're old enough to drink, right?"

"Kidnapping me *and* trying to get me drunk?"

I grin, hooking my arm around his chair so I can see behind the car. "I don't half-ass anything."

The ride is quiet, with both of us just listening to the music. When I look over at Griffin, he's watching the scenery pass by. As somebody who grew up in the Midwest, where it's winter three quarters of the year, I can appreciate the view. Eastshore is, predictably, right on the east shore. A little south of Jacksonville. It's a pretty small town with a lot of history. At least it was

34

before the college blew up. The athletics department really put it on the map, and now it's a certified college town in its own right.

And that means plenty of bars.

The Tigers' Den is the requisite college-themed sports bar on the downtown strip. Surrounded by ancient buildings made out of coquina, the Den definitely stands out. It's got the same sort of rustic finish, but the inside is all neon and typical bar atmosphere. There's at least a terrace to make the place look respectable, but none of the Eastshore guys actually use it.

The door's propped open, and as Griffin and I pull up, I can hear my teammates inside. Right now, the college is still between semesters, so it's just us here, working our asses off. I lead Griffin in, greet the guys I'm used to seeing here, and find us a booth. Everybody seems pretty happy with their own tables, and to my surprise, nobody invites themselves to sit it ours.

It's a good thing, considering the fact that I need Griffin to be real with me.

"Nice place. I think part of my shoe is permanently stuck to the floor."

I laugh, lifting my own shoe off of the tacky floor. "Yeah, college bar. What are you gonna do?"

"Hey, I get it. My dorm floor is usually the same way."

"What building are you in?"

"Masterson."

"Ah, shit. I was there last year. Know exactly what you mean. That and all the fucking stains on the walls."

Griffin laughs. "Thanks, man. I almost forgot about those."

"No problem."

A server comes to our table, and I put in an order for a cheeseburger and a pitcher of whatever's on tap, then let Griffin get his own order in. The server heads back to the kitchen, and I briefly flick my gaze to the TV, then back to him.

"This is on me, by the way."

"You don't have to do that. Really. You offering to work with me is... More than enough."

I don't know why, but the sincerity in his voice catches me off guard.

"Bringing you up helps the whole team."

"Yeah, but you could just as easily let me ride the bench. That would've only affected me, not the team."

I shrugged. "Maybe. But I think benching you would be a waste."

The pitcher comes and I pour us both a glass. The familiar tickle of the foam is almost like a rush all by itself as I raise the glass to my lips. I take a drink, and it clings to my skin. Before I can wipe it away, I see Griffin staring at me, his gaze fixated on my lips. Another strange feeling flutters low in my gut, and I shift a little in my seat.

I can't even manage ribbing him right now. Instead, I wipe my mouth with the back of my hand, and Griffin quickly turns his attention to the TV. We both watch for a while, complaining about the same shitty call on a baseball game. I'm not a huge fan, but it's a distraction. And it's not like there's much else to watch when it isn't football season.

Once I pour us both a refill I figure it's about time to get down to business. "So. What is it you're afraid of?"

"Needles. Plague. Mice kind of freak me out, to be honest with you."

I roll my eyes, but a smirk tugs at my lips. "Very funny, smart ass. Is it the pain?"

"No, I'm not worried about the pain." From the expression on his face and the brief shadow the passes across his eyes, I'm willing to bet he's experienced a lot more pain than the kind a skilled defender can dole out. " It's... Kind of a long story."

"I got time."

With all the other football players here ordering the exact same thing, we're still waiting our meal anyway. But I don't pressure him. Instead, I lean my elbow against the table and take another drink of my beer. It takes a hell of a lot to get me drunk, but I'm starting to feel a tiny buzz.

"I was injured back in high school." Both his hands are around his glass, and he looks down at the table when he says it.

"No shit? Torn ligament? Hairline fracture?"

Injury is a big part of football, but I'm not going to be the asshole who says that right now. Nobody likes to be laid out on the field. I've been there, and it definitely fucks with your head. For me, every sack rockets my anxiety up to 11. Every time my back hits the grass, I wonder if it's going to be the last time I take the field.

And I haven't even gotten hit with a concussion yet.

"Paralysis, actually."

That gets my attention. My gaze snaps up to him, and there's no hint of a joke in his eyes. Not that anybody would joke about that.

"Temporary. I guess that's obvious, though. Got hit just the right way that it shifted one of the discs in my back. Put pressure on the spinal cord, made my legs useless for a while."

I can feel my jaw move as I try to form words, but it takes a few attempts to get them out. "Shit. Did you just eventually get feeling back in your legs?"

"Yeah, after about four months. Took longer to relearn how to use them."

"When did this happen?"

"Junior year of high school."

"So what, four of five years ago? And you're already playing ball again? Jesus, man."

I can't even imagine. Even just having to go through physical therapy after fucking up my shoulder was a big deal for me. You never realize how much your body works to move things until you mess something up. All of the practices I've been through, all of the drills I've run, and those six weeks were still the most intense of my life.

But learning to walk again? Getting to the point where you can actually play a sport like football? My respect for Griffin just multiplied tenfold.

"Yeah. The physical stuff is pretty much behind me, and I thought the mental was, too.

Guess not."

Any normal person would probably tell him to cut himself some slack. But I don't think that's what he wants to hear, and that's not who I am.

"We'll figure it out," I say as the server brings our burgers.

We talk about sports between mouthfuls, and I scratch out a plan on a cocktail napkin. Derek Griffin put in the time, and he deserves to get past this. There's no way I could ever do anything close to what he did, and I want to have a part in it. I want to help him get his comeback. He deserves it.

CHAPTER FIVE
- Derek -

People usually have one of two reactions when I tell them about my injury. The overwhelming one is pity, but every now and again there's someone who seems to understand exactly what it takes to come back from something like that. Hawk's in the latter camp, and he doesn't give me any bullshit about how I was robbed, or how it's a miracle I'm even walking now. He understands. I don't just want to walk. I want to play football.

Hell, if I'm being completely honest with myself, I want things to go back to the way they were before I got injured. Before I realized there were people in this world so fucking hateful that they would do something like that.

Of course, I don't tell Hawk any of that. It's not completely unbelievable that such a serious injury would randomly happen on a football field, so I'm not too worried about him asking questions. I guess I should feel more ashamed, since he's offering to help me. But I just can't. Some secrets I have to keep with me. And maybe I'm holding myself back by doing it, but I can't really imagine letting anybody else know this.

Right now, I can pretend it was just another run-of-the-mill injury, and that I'm terrified of it happening again. It's not exactly a lie, it's just not the whole truth.

With my burger finished, I get to work on my fries. Everything tastes amazing, but after working so hard earlier today, my stomach is feeling a little unsettled. Of course, it could be a side effect of drinking so much beer before eating anything. I've always been a lightweight, from the time my friends and I were sneaking beers out of our parents' fridge in junior high.

I'm never gonna be a big party guy, and I'm okay with that.

Hawk is going to town, though. He's downed most of the pitcher himself, and I'm glad he hasn't noticed that I haven't kept up with him yet. Considering how big he is, he can probably put down a lot before he even thinks about it. And it's not my place to question what he does.

Not like he's my boyfriend.

Jesus. One day of him talking to me and my subconscious is already fantasizing. Great.

I watch him scribble something on a napkin, and my curiosity gets the better of me. Eventually he slides it across the table, and I squint as I look at it. It's a schedule. Written in surprisingly neat, elegant handwriting. Totally unexpected coming from the guy sitting across from me.

"What's this?"

"Your new schedule. It'll probably have to change around a bit, if Coach calls practice on the fly. But right now, these are the times we'll work one-on-one. I can get some extra time on the field, or we can hit up the park. Your choice."

He's got sessions slotted out every other day, at least. I have a feeling this is going to have to change once classes start, but right now I find myself almost a little giddy at the idea of spending so much time with him. And this is while he's going to force me to get tackled over and over again. The only thing my treacherous mind can think is that I hope he's the one doing the tackling.

"You sure you have time for all this?"

"Yeah. Not a whole lot to do before the semester starts. And I want to get as much work in as possible. If you want to start this season, you'll have to impress Coach Garvey pretty quick."

"Well... Thanks, man."

His lips turn up in a grin. "You sound surprised."

"I am. I mean, you don't know me. At all. You don't know my stats from high school, you don't know if I was just having a good run in practice today. And you're willing to spend the time to help fix me."

He finishes a bite and locks eyes with me. I can't help it. I'm caught in the intensity of his stare, his light blue eyes both calming and exhilarating.

"Anybody who can come back from an injury like that is worth fixing."

And just like that, the discussion is over. Even if I have no idea why someone like Hawk would do this for me, I can't help but trust him. He's putting himself out there, giving me some of his precious time. A *lot* of his time, if this napkin is anything to go by. So trusting him is the least I can do.

When Hawk turns his attention back to the TV, I turn my attention to him. He cuts a profile like a Greek statue, all hard lines and perfection. Strong jaw, nicely squared face, and a brow that's masculine but not reaching Neanderthal levels. When he smiles, or when he focuses, his sky-blue eyes crinkle just a little bit in the corners. In 20 years, he's going to be one of those gorgeous guys who has laugh lines carved into his face.

Not that he isn't already gorgeous.

It's his lips that really get me, though. His mouth is framed by rough stubble that outlines the shadow of a beard. But his lips look soft and full. I've always been a sucker for a guy who can kiss, and with lips like that, I'm willing to bet Hawk is pretty damn good at it.

But what are the chances of me ever finding out? Pretty fucking slim.

As soon as the question forms on the tip of my tongue, I know I shouldn't ask it. Even if I couch it between a few more reasonable questions, it's not like he and I are best buds. I shouldn't be thinking about what it would feel like to kiss him, but right now, it's the only thing keeping me from thinking about what it felt like to lay broken on the ground, and not be able to feel my legs.

"So you're a senior, right?" Safe question number one.

He takes a drink of his beer before answering. The pitcher's almost polished off now.

"Yeah. Fifth year, actually. Went a little light in the class load a couple years back."

Considering how dedicated he seems to football, I'm not surprised. "What's your major?"

"Communication."

"You trying to be a sportscaster or something?"

He shrugs, turning his attention back to the TV. "I guess if a professional career doesn't pan out, yeah."

His shoulders are tense, and his posture is completely closed off. Apparently I've already touched on a sore spot, and I haven't even asked I really want to know.

"Where are you staying until the dorms open up?"

"My dad got an apartment down here. We lived in Michigan before this, and after my mom died, he didn't really have any reason to stay. Gives him a chance to keep an eye on me, too." He says it offhandedly, but there's still a little tension and him.

"Sorry about your mom."

He just nods, then pours the last of the pitcher into his glass. "You want another?"

"I'm good."

I'm starting to think that Jason Hawkins is a more complicated guy than I first suspected. And that any question I ask him is going to have a complicated answer.

"So what do you guys usually do outside of football?"

"There's something outside of football?" That makes him chuckle, like he's finally comfortable with the conversation again. "Not a whole lot. There's this place, and there's always some party going on somewhere. The guys who live in the same dorm like to get together and play

Madden. Other than that, can't say there's a whole lot going on during the season."

He's still not really talking about himself. I know I shouldn't pry, but I just can't help myself.

"Must be hard to date with a schedule like that. Your girl okay with you spending so much time on the field?"

Hawk looks back at me, and for a second I think he's going to call me on my bullshit. My heart is thumping hard in my chest, and I swear there's no way he can't hear it. But he just shrugs, then looks away.

"She wasn't. That's why we broke up. Two years ago." He takes another sip of his beer before continuing. "Thought I could balance a social life with everything else, but it just didn't work out."

There's a part of me that's deliriously happy to hear he doesn't have a girlfriend right now. Of course, that part of me is completely ignoring the fact that he's obviously straight. Not that I didn't know that going into this. Whatever *this* is. I feel like I'm back in junior high, passing a note to someone I like.

"I feel you. Don't really get out much myself."

Back when I was seeing a therapist, she suggested it was because of anxiety. Whether that developed after my injury, or before it, I'll never know. But at least it gives Hawk and I something to bond over, in a roundabout way.

He lifts his glass in invitation, and I clink mine against his.

"At least I'm not the only pathetic one out

here."

I laugh. "Glad to be of service."

I don't ask him anything more about his personal life, and he doesn't really seem interested in mine. We watch the rest of the inning, and see the Mets shut out the Cardinals. A few displeased groans and shouts come from the tables around us, and I see beer money change hands. Once SportsCenter comes on, Hawk fishes out his wallet and pays for the meal, just like he said he would. I want to argue again, but for the sake of my finances, I know I shouldn't. It's hard enough having to pay either for gas or a hotel room until the dorms open up again.

With the bill settled, Hawk stands up and sways a little, catching himself on his chair. From the expression on his face, I'm guessing he didn't realize how quickly he downed those beers. I'm surprised he hasn't had to wander off for a piss or two by now.

"Shit. I'm gonna have to call a cab. I can drop you off wherever."

Leave it to Hawk to be the one responsible college student in this bar. I want to offer to drive him back so he doesn't have to waste even more money on my account, but I've got a bit of a head rush, too. And I don't have any desire to be scraped off the asphalt.

"Don't worry about it. I can walk."

"You sure?"

"Yeah. Bus stop isn't far from here."

He nods, and before he can pull out some cash for the tip, I beat him to it. A small smile is my reward, and it's definitely reward enough.

"Remember the schedule," he says, tapping his finger on the napkin.

I pick up the napkin and slip it into my pocket. At this point, there's no chance of me forgetting.

CHAPTER SIX
- Jason -

The first few training sessions go pretty well. Griff is a hard worker, just like I guessed. And even the sessions scheduled just a couple hours after practice get his full attention and effort.

If everybody on the team took it as seriously as him, there's no way we wouldn't get a seat in the top four.

I'm still a little blown away by what he told me. Watching him move, seeing the way he pivots and cuts across the field, sprints and breaks away from defenders, there's no way I would've ever guessed he suffered an injury that bad.

And yeah, I'll admit I had to look it up. It's not that I didn't believe him. The guy seems trustworthy. I just wanted to see if it made the news back in his hometown.

What I found was pretty fucking chilling.

Griff is from a small town in Texas. He's said it's exactly like Austin, except everybody is stuck in the same ass backwards mindset, and the music totally sucks. Oh, and there are a few thousand less people, and three times the churches per square mile.

The article I found online was published in 2010. He played as a receiver for the Brighton Bobcats, and wasn't far off from being considered as an All-American. If he would've been able to complete his senior year, it seems like he would've been a shoe in.

But while his stats are impressive, it's the details of his injury that catch my attention. The article said that it was an accident, but the video that accompanies it says otherwise.

It's grainy as hell, and shot from somewhere high up in the stands. The first time I watched it, I heard the contact more than saw it. Hell, I felt it, deep down in my bones. My own back started to ache as I saw Griff just lying there on the ground, not moving.

But the second time I watched, I noticed something more than an overly aggressive tackle.

Griff's blocker slowed down. He was keeping time with him, but as soon as the safety started to put on speed, he slowed down. Didn't even try to get the block.

And the tackle wasn't just a case of getting a bad angle. That guy had every chance in the world to line it up, but he chose to go for the hit that would make the biggest impact. He chose to grab Griff low, crushing his helmet into Griff's back. Just watching it made me grind my teeth, and the more I played it back, the more pissed off I got.

If it *was* intentional, though, that's one more reason for me to admire him. He's getting out there, coming back from one of the worst things that could happen in high school football, and even though I can tell he's about one step away from shitting bricks, he seems to trust me enough to let me help.

I researched the topic online, and ran my plan by Coach Garvey. My goal was to set up a controlled environment in which Griff could take a tackle on his terms. Coach was impressed, and so far, it seems to be working out.

I've had a few friends help me. Mills, West, and Carter. They're all pretty big guys, and definitely imposing. We've worked on the field, with me setting up passes and the other guys running interference. The first time, they just got close and put pressure on him.

Even then, I could see him go pale. His legs locked up and he dropped like a stone. One thing I can say in his favor, though—he made sure to protect the ball. The guys gave him hell, getting up in his face, trying to bat it away from him, but he never let go.

Gradually he got more comfortable with that, and after a while we started doing contact. I told the guys to take it easy, but Mills got a little enthusiastic. By the time we were through, Griff had more grass stains on his practice jersey than a peewee player with untied shoes. None of the guys did a full tackle, but everybody was definitely winded by the end of the session.

The five of us grab a table at the Den, along with a couple pitchers and two large pizzas. West and Carter pull up extra chairs, and it's almost comical how small Griff and I look next to the linebackers.

It's Friday night, and Coach is laying off the practice for the weekend. Even I'm grateful for a little break. The other guys must be, too, because those pitchers are disappearing fast, and so is the pizza.

"Okay, best quarterback of all time?"

It's just the next in a long line of opinion questions Mills has asked, and just like the rest, there's no way it's going to end well.

"And if you say Brady, I swear to God I will kick your ass."

"What's wrong with Brady?" West takes the bait.

I cringe. "Don't ask, man."

"Marino," Carter says, raising his glass to his lips.

Wrong answer. I can already tell by the way Mills leans over the table.

"Are you fucking kidding me? Marino doesn't even have a ring."

"Still has the most completions," Griff says.

"Dude, don't encourage him." Mills leans across the table and punches Griff in the arm.

For some reason it feels good to see Griff getting along with the guys. Taking and giving shit. I guess it feels like hope. If he can survive typical locker room bullshit, he can survive out on the field.

"And yards and TDs."

The debate continues for a while, with Mills rejecting everything but his own pick. I give my input—Montana, of course, which Mills says is predictable, even if Griff agrees with me—and we finish off our beers. It's pretty crowded at the Den tonight, and for once we're not surrounded by other football players. The guys who don't have a place to stay around town have probably already gone home for the weekend.

Around midnight or so, West and Carter get

into a heated battle at the air hockey table. Mills, lightweight that he is, checks out. It's just me and Griff left, and I'm starting to feel a serious need to ditch this place.

"You heading home for the weekend?" I ask.

"Planned on it, but my gran's playing in a bridge tournament Kissimmee. Apparently she's hot shit," he says with a smile that shows off his dimples. "Won't be home all weekend, so it would just be me, stuck in the middle of a retirement community."

"And spending the weekend being asked to clean out gutters and lift heavy boxes isn't your idea of fun?"

"You got it," he says, lifting his glass up.

"Shit, have you been driving all the way back to Kissimmee every day?"

That's got to be at least a four hour drive round trip.

"Nah, staying in a motel." I must make a face or something, because he continues. "It's not that bad. Makes me grateful the bank practically begged me to sign up for a credit card as a freshman."

"Why don't you come stay at my place this weekend."

The offer comes out before I even really think about making it, but... I'm okay with it. I haven't had anybody over since high school, and that was back in Michigan, but I'm sure Dad won't mind. He loves football players. Especially other guys who play offense. And I've told him about

Griff, so he already knows his story.

"What, like a training thing?"

I shrug. "Like a hanging out thing."

It's been a while since I've taken a weekend to kick back. At least since the end of last season, if I had to guess. Dad will be all over me Monday morning, but I think he'll understand. And it's not like I'm a kid anymore.

"Yeah. Sure. If your Dad's cool with it."

"He'll be fine. Let me finish this up and we'll get outta here."

Ten minutes later, we head out. Usually it makes me anxious to even think about spending a weekend not working on my form or at least putting in some serious time at the gym, but this time I'm actually looking forward to it.

CHAPTER SEVEN
- Derek -

When we make it up to Hawk's apartment, I feel like an imposter.

I don't know why. I guess it's because he's only known me for a couple weeks. I'm not going to complain, but it makes me wonder if Hawk hangs out with anyone outside of practice and the Den, or if he's just giving me a break because I'm the poor, homeless new kid.

Okay, so maybe the homeless part isn't true. My parents are back in Texas, and my grandma told me a million times she's fine with me staying at her place even if she isn't there. But the rest of it still stands.

Plus, I'm a little nervous about meeting his dad.

As Hawk fishes out a key, I feel like I should be thinking up some kind of excuse for why I kept his son out so late. And why he still kinda smells like beer. But Hawk's a grown ass man, and his dad probably doesn't care what he does or who he does it with.

Hawk flicks the light on as soon as he gets inside, and I step in behind him to see a pretty decent apartment. Definitely a bachelor pad. Sparse on furniture. Looks like most of it is from IKEA, but I can't judge. There's a shirt on the back of the couch that Hawk picks up, and a Heineken bottle sitting out on an end table that he also snags, but other than that it's not too messy.

"My room's down the hall, second on the

right. Bathroom's all the way at the end if you gotta take a piss."

Hawk goes to take care of the shirt and bottle, and I make my way down the hallway, trying not to make a big deal out of the fact that I'm going to be staying in his room. This isn't high school. I'm not sneaking upstairs with him and trying to keep quiet while he palms me through my jeans.

Not that I'd mind...

Loud snoring from across the hall breaks me out of my stupid little fantasy, and I hang a right into Hawk's room. It's tidy, but pretty Spartan. More than the rest of the apartment. The essential pieces of furniture are there, but nothing really feels lived in. No decorations on the walls, and even the area around his computer is pretty clean.

Then again, he's got to be twenty-two or twenty-three, at least. Not like I'm going to find posters of some supermodel plastered on the ceiling and a waste basket filled with used tissues.

After that distracting thought, Hawk comes in behind me and closes the door. "There's a roll-away in the closet. Up to you if you want to take that or the bed. Doesn't matter to me either way."

"I'm cool with the roll-away. You're the one who's letting me stay here."

He chucks his bag into the corner and starts over toward the closet. It's a small room, about the size of an average dorm room, and I have to make space for him. That doesn't stop him from accidentally brushing against me as he goes past, and a little shiver races up my spine at the contact. Apparently I had way too much beer at the Den. It's messing with my judgment.

"Need a hand?"

"I got it," he says, lifting the roll-away out of the closet.

He sets it up on the floor beside his bed, then stands above it, raking a hand through his hair.

"You need a blanket or anything? I can toss you an extra pillow for my bed."

"Nah, I'm good."

He nods, then blows out of breath through mostly closed lips. He seems a little nervous, and it's definitely endearing. Even if I know he isn't having the same thoughts I am. He just doesn't strike me as a guy who has a lot of people over to his place. And if he ever did, it was probably back in Michigan.

"You don't have to entertain me or anything, man. I'm just grateful for a place to crash."

He lets out a relieved laugh. "It obvious I don't do this all that often?"

"Not exactly a social butterfly myself."

He nods again and then makes a face. As I watch him, he tugs the collar of his shirt up to his nose and inhales. "My clothes smell like beer. Need to change. You mind?"

I don't know why he's asking. It's not like he doesn't change in front of tons of guys in the locker room. But I guess being at his house is different. Maybe he thinks I'll somehow be offended if he doesn't leave his own room and go into the bathroom to change. He's definitely wrong about that.

"Go for it. I can turn around if you want. Cover my eyes," I tease.

"Very funny."

He pulls some fresh clothes out of his dresser, and I wonder if he'd feel the same way if he knew I was gay. I've had friends who didn't care, but for the most part, the guys I played with always seemed really uncomfortable getting undressed around me. Probably thought I would see one flash of skin and lose my fucking mind.

But it doesn't work like that.

Of course, as soon as Hawk strips off his shirt, I start to regret my decision. He has his back turned to me, and I have a full, indulgent view of his muscles as they flex and tense. He's not insanely built, but *something* ripples whenever he moves, drawing my attention in an unabashed stare. I want him to turn around so I can see his chest, but I don't want him to see me watching him. It's definitely a problem, and now I'm kicking myself for having some holier than thou attitude about not being immediately drawn to guys who take their clothes off.

But I'm around half naked—and sometimes fully naked—guys almost every day in the locker room and the showers. It's just Hawk that makes me this way. Turns me into the kind of creep who stares lustfully at a guy who's only trying to help him.

As he tugs down his jeans, I turn my head

60

away. I doubt he'll strip beyond his underwear, but even that's too much temptation. Way too likely that he'll catch me checking out his ass, and there's no way I can cover that up. Not much chance of hiding a boner if it happens, either.

Oh, who am I kidding. *When* it happens.

"If you aren't tired yet, I can fire up the Xbox. I don't have a ton of games, but I've got the newest copy of Madden."

A smile quirks my lips. Not that long ago, Hawk complained about the guys who hang around in the dorm rooms and play video games all day. Either he's a little jealous, or he just doesn't get home that often. Considering there's a light layer of dust on top of his console, I'm guessing it's the latter.

"Yeah, that'd be cool."

Hawk finishes changing, and I realize I've only really got my gym clothes in my bag. A few shower supplies, too, but not the stuff I'd need to stay the weekend. He'll have to drop me by the hotel tomorrow morning. As I'm trying to decide whether I should change, Hawk sits on the edge of the bed and fires up the Xbox. He doesn't exactly invite me there, but there aren't a lot of places to sit, so it's either there or the floor. Against my better judgment, I take a seat beside him, leaving enough space between us to still be cool. But my heart is racing the whole time, and I can practically feel the heat of his body beside me. My mind starts to conjure images of Hawk reaching over, sliding his hand over my thigh, giving me that look, and then pushing me back on the bed and having his way with me.

Shit. This is *not* the way to avoid a boner.

We play a couple games, and I try to keep it together. I suck at Madden under regular circumstances, but doubly so when I'm thinking of anything but the game. Every time it's Hawk's turn, I check out his profile as he concentrates on the screen. He has an adorable habit of licking his lips when he's deep in concentration, and it's killing me. Slowly but surely.

He kicks my ass easily, and once the controllers are set aside, he gives me a strange look. His brow is furrowed, his lips are parted, and I can tell he wants to say something. Again my heart speeds, and I wonder if he's going to call me out from looking at him so much.

"Derek, I gotta be straight with you, man."

I really wish you wouldn't.

"I know what happened to you in high school. I saw the video."

I can practically feel the relief flood my body, but it's also mixed with a chaser of disappointment. I guess some part of me is still hoping that, against all odds, Hawk has this deeply hidden desire to experiment with his sexuality. Oh well.

"I forgot that even existed. Used to watch it for hours on end after I got out of the hospital. Shit messed me up."

"I bet. I just... Wanted to see what you're dealing with. And I may be way off base here, but it looked like that hit wasn't just a regular tackle."

My breath catches in my throat, and it's like

my lungs suddenly stop, threatening to strangle me. Is he really asking what I think he is? It's been years, and nobody has ever seen through that clip. Then again, it takes a football player to know what another is thinking, and it's not like it's been on anyone's must-watch list beyond some morbid fascination with seeing another person's pain.

I have to make a decision, and quick. He's going to ask questions, and it's probably better if I just throw it all out there and let him deal with it the way he wants. But there's a part of me that's afraid of his reaction. Either he'll move firmly into the camp of pitying me, or he'll start to distance himself from me. Both options suck, but I don't want to lie to him, either. In a very short time, Hawk has become a friend. I think he could be a really good friend, and I don't want to fuck that up.

My parents used to tell me that anyone who decides they don't like me because of who and what I am isn't worth knowing, anyway. But they're my parents. They have to say shit like that. It's harder to think about it that way when you're faced with the prospect of losing a friend.

I swallow down the lump in my throat, and make my decision.

"That's because it wasn't."

He doesn't say anything, just lets out a breath like he was holding it in, waiting for my answer. He nods slowly, and whether he's just taking time to process it, or actively giving me time to compose my thoughts, it's appreciated.

"I told you I lived in a small town. Not the

most open-minded place in the world, and anything that happens there gets around within a week." There were times when I feared for my life in that town, and that's part of why I ultimately decided to go to college out of state. "My junior year, I started having to... Face some hard facts about myself. I wanted to live my life and stop being afraid. To figure out if my hunch was true."

I'd been on dates before that. With girls, obviously. I even had sex before that, though it was awkward as hell and pretty much confirmed the fact that I'm 100% gay. I don't know what came over me that year, but I'd just had enough.

"I'm gay, man. I came out to my parents that year, and I the team found out about it a couple months later."

That's not the whole truth. I think about the offensive tackle in that video—the one who deliberately missed his block—and I feel my stomach lurch. I could've dealt with just being harassed and called a fag by the rest of my teammates. I could've even dealt with the injury, deliberate or not. But the way it happened...

Hawk sinks back into the bed for a moment, and I venture a glance at him. I can practically see the wheels turning, and I wait for him to put it together.

"He didn't block for you. He could've easily taken that guy out, and he didn't." There's a severity to his voice that surprises me. "That's fucked up."

Can argue with that. "Yep."

"Seriously, Derek. That's really fucked up."

He stands, pacing in the small space between me and the TV. One hand covers his chin and his mouth, and the other is holding his elbow. He actually looks a little torn up about this, and I don't know what to say. I guess I didn't expect him to be completely unsympathetic, or to be an asshole about it, but this looks like something more than pity. Honestly, the overwhelming emotion I'm reading from him his anger.

He stops in front of me, and his eyes are a little wild. "Did you file charges?"

"What? No, I didn't file charges. What was I going to say? I was tackled on a football field, Jason." It doesn't feel right to use his nickname right now. And since he's actually using my given name, too, I guess this makes us even on the familiarity scales. "There's no way I would've ever had a case. I just wanted it to go away."

He sits back down again, and the bed jostles beneath me. As I watch him, he rakes a hand through his hair and lets out a hefty sigh. "Sorry. That shit just gets to me."

"It's okay," I say quietly, not knowing what else I can offer. This definitely isn't the reaction I expected from him.

"No, it's not. I had a friend in high school. Nathan. We went to different colleges, and the first year I was here, I found out he got the shit beat out of him behind some bar. Some guys thought he was hitting on them."

Now it's my turn to look surprised. "Shit. Was he okay?"

"Yeah. Spent the night in the hospital. They

broke a few ribs, and he had to get stitches. But he was okay." Hawk—Jason—hangs his head down past his shoulders, putting both hands on the back of it.

"People are really shitty."

I came into this thinking that if I ever told him I was gay, I'd have to offer him an out. Give him an easy way to put some distance between us. But knowing Hawk has a friend who's gay puts me at ease. Even if what happened to him is terrible.

"Yeah, they are." He lifts his head a little to look at me. "If anybody on the team even starts to give you shit, you tell me, okay? I'm not going to let this happen again."

A flutter makes its way through my chest, and I have to remind myself he's only defending me because he feels guilty for what happened to his friend. "Sure. But it's not really something I want to broadcast to the team. If they find out, they find out. You're the first person at Eastshore who knows, aside from my roommates."

"Nobody will hear it from me."

It's easy to believe him. Jason Hawkins doesn't exactly seem like a gossip, and he looks like he's trying to atone for past sins. It rankles me a little, but beggars can't exactly be choosers. At this point, I'm just glad I'm not going to lose him as a friend over this.

Now I just need to get my head on straight and stop fantasizing about him.

He doesn't ask me any more questions, and we both get settled into our respective beds. I'm glad for the quiet. There are some things I'm just not ready to talk about. As I lay on my back, staring up at the ceiling fan, on top of a roll-away that's a little too small for me, I think about what it would be like to tell Hawk everything. We're not there yet. But maybe someday we could be.

CHAPTER EIGHT
- Jason -

I don't know what time it is when my door slams open.

It's Sunday morning, I know that at least. Griff's been here for one day, and my dad had him watching his favorite tapes from past seasons. We cooked a few stakes in the backyard, and had an okay time. Griff and I headed out to the Y to play some hoops, and when we got back, dad was gone. Probably hit the bar, but I'm not his keeper, so I didn't worry about it.

I guess I should worry about it now.

"What the fuck is this?"

It's the first thing I hear, yanking me violently out of a dream. My heart pounds as I sit straight up in bed. I try to catch my breath, feeling like I've just run a marathon, but he isn't giving me the chance. He shoves a folded paper in my face, and my eyes are still bleary from sleep. I can't make out what it says.

"Answer me, Jason. What is this?"

I hear Griff rustle on the roll-away beside me, and my stomach lurches. I can't smell any alcohol on Dad's breath, but he's pissed as hell. Taking the paper, I squint and try to make sense of it, hoping if I give him an answer he'll leave me alone.

It's a list of the classes I'm taking this semester. Eastshore always sends them out the week before classes start so we can get our books and anything else we need. As I look it over, I realize what he's angry about.

"Can we do this somewhere else?"

"No, we do this here. Now."

Out of the corner of my eye, I see Griff sit up. He blinks away the sleep, and I hope he isn't awake enough to realize what's going on.

"Sorry," I say to him. He just gives me a sympathetic look. "You mind getting the coffee started this morning?"

"The coffee can wait," Dad says, in a voice that makes Griff stop moving. "Right now, you're going to tell me why you're only taking three classes this semester when you need 15 credits to graduate."

"I can't fit in 15 credits with football. You know that."

He rips the paper out of my hands. "No, I don't know that. I know you're supposed to be a full-time student at that school. That you're supposed to graduate this year. Hell, I know you were supposed to graduate last year, and I already gave you slack for that, Jason."

Bullshit. He's been on my ass about that since he found out.

"What do you expect me to do? When I'm not at school or practice, you've got me working drills here or at the park. When am I supposed to do schoolwork?"

His face is red, and his brows draw close together. "Don't you put this on me. It's your responsibility to do well in school."

"So what do you want me to do?" I repeat, knowing I'm treading on thin ice.

"Monday morning, you tell them to fit you into two more classes this semester. I don't care what they are, but you're getting those credits."

My teeth grind together and my chest feels tight and heavy. It's anxiety, I know. This feeling of helplessness I always get around him. My dads never beat me. He's given me everything I've ever wanted. But this is the same old song and dance we've always done. He wants to push me. Wants me to push myself. I get so close to the breaking point, and when I step back from the ledge to keep from falling, he just pushes me out there again.

It's overwhelming, and right now, someone else is witnessing every bit of it.

"This isn't a negotiation, Jason."

"And what if I don't? What if I can't handle it, and I need to take three classes this semester instead of five?"

I know he won't make me quit football. He's never even threatened it, because he knows I wouldn't take it seriously. Football is everything to him.

"You want to test me, boy? Your scholarship ends this year, Jason. In case you haven't noticed, we're not exactly drowning in money over here. So you want to draw it out, go right ahead. But don't expect me to pay your way, and don't expect NFL recruiters to wait for you."

He crumples up the paper and throws it on my bed. Storming toward my door, he flings it open, and I see his shoulders rise and fall as he takes in a deep breath. He turns, ignoring me completely, and looks at Griff who's still sitting frozen atop the roll-away.

"Sorry you had to see that. You're welcome to stay as long as you want."

He pulls the door shut behind him, a little harder than necessary, but not with the slam I expected. Letting out a deep breath, I stare at the ceiling and wish I could go back in time. Years in time, before Dad became obsessed with this. Maybe back to when Mom was still alive, because she was always able to talk sense into him. With her around, I usually didn't feel like I was on the verge of a nervous breakdown every second.

Right now, though, I just want the chance to rewind time and find some way to get Griff out of here before he sees that.

He hasn't said anything, and I know I'm going to have to be the first one to bring it up. Might as well rip that bandage off now. "Sorry about that. I should've told him before he found out this way."

"It's okay. Is he always so... intense?"

I laugh, but it's the kind of laugh you do to keep from feeling anything else. "Yeah. He means well, I guess. I wouldn't be where I am today if it wasn't for him."

Griff doesn't say anything, and I look over at him to get some idea of what he's thinking. His gaze meets mine, and I see the question there. He's asking if I really believe that, and I don't have an answer.

"Football is a big deal to him. To me. He knows if I don't graduate this year, I'm either going to have to quit school before I get a degree, or skip the draft."

"Five classes is a lot to take in a semester when you're doing as much as he has you doing."

I just nod. I already know that. That's why I signed up for three.

"So what was your plan?"

My defenses fire off, and it's on the tip of my tongue to snap back at him. But it isn't an accusation. I can hear it in his voice. He just genuinely wants to know.

"I don't know. Double up in the summer, maybe. Take night classes or something with a lab to get extra credits. I really don't know."

I let out a long sigh. My whole body is tense, caught between wanting to get the hell out of here, and wanting to just curl up and go back to bed. That's what my life has been like at Eastshore so far. Nobody in the world knows that, and right now my biggest fear is that Derek Griffin is starting to figure it out.

I guess I'd better head him off at the pass.

"I looked at the catalog over the summer. Tried to find classes I thought would be easy. But I just stared at those last two spaces." I remember feeling physical pain as I thought about the pressure of trying to juggle that much football and that many classes. "It was a stupid decision, but I couldn't put two more on there."

I hear Griff let out a sigh of his own, and when I glance down at him, his brows are knit together. He looks at me, then away. "You're not going to like what I have to say."

"I don't like much of anything about this

day right now, so it can't get any worse."

"I think you need to register for those last two classes. You need to tell your dad that you have enough time in practice to get everything done when it comes to football."

I let out a dry laugh. "Yeah. That'll go over well."

"It's either that or you don't graduate. And what happens if you're injured in the NFL? What happens when your career ends? I know your dad wants your life to be nothing but football, but what do you want?"

Nobody's ever really asked me that. Sure, maybe a high school counselor. Once. But from an early age, my life plan was pretty much laid out before me. I never had a problem with it. I love football. It's the only thing I'm good at, and the only thing I'm ever going to be good at.

But something changed in college. I don't know if life just got harder, or I got weaker. It started to overwhelm me, and now I feel like it could all unravel at any moment.

I'm scared shitless of that happening. And I don't really have an answer to Griff's question.

"I don't know."

I want things to be easy like they were when I was a kid. When getting to train all day with my dad was a dream, and not something that constantly beats me down. But that's never going to happen.

"I'll help you with school. I've kept up a 3.9 GPA for my first two years here, and I don't really have any commitments outside of football. Sign up

for those two classes, and we'll figure it out.
Okay?"

"I don't need your sympathy, Griffin. I can
figure it out on my own."

"Yeah, no. It sounds like you been trying to
figure it out on your own for a long time. And who
the fuck doesn't need sympathy?"

When I look over at him, he offers me a
small smile. I try to match it, but I only feel my
lips move the tiniest bit.

"Come on. We can walk to Denny's from
here. I'll buy a breakfast."

I can't say no to a big plate of greasy bacon
and overcooked eggs. But it's mostly the fact that
Griff is willing to put this shit behind us. Only one
thing holds me back from immediately accepting
his offer.

"Hey... I don't really want this getting out.
Nobody else knows."

Griff just shrugs. "No problem. You keep
my secret, I'll keep yours." He smiles again, and
those damn dimples come back. This time, a weird
little flutter in my stomach accompanies them.
"You wanna pinky swear on it?"

I reach up and shove at his arm. He barely
moves. "Asshole."

But he's got me smiling for real this time.
And laughing, too. It's not that this shit gets me so
down that I don't feel like I can be happy, but I'm
not used to being able to bounce back so quick
after getting hammered by my dad's
disappointment. As we get ready to go, I start to
feel a little more comfortable with Griff knowing

my secrets. He's a good guy. Somehow I already know I can trust him. And it's been a long time since I've had somebody to lean on.

Maybe that's what's been missing from my life.

SEPTEMBER

CHAPTER NINE
- Jason -

After weeks of working with him, I find out Griff isn't going to start in Saturday's game.

I knew it was a long shot going into it. Coach Garvey pretty much confirmed that when I talked to him. But it still pisses me off that I wasn't able to make enough of a difference. I know Griff worked hard. Hell, he put in more time and effort than almost everybody who actually *is* starting. All the guys who helped him agree.

"I can talk to the coach. Might still be time to change things around."

Griffin and I have gone back to our respective lockers. The guys usually between us are in the showers, so I've got a direct line to talk to him for once.

"We don't need a *Rudy* moment where you lay your jersey on Coach's desk, man."

I grin, shaking my head. That's the first thing that popped into my head, too. "Yeah, well. Let me know if you change your mind."

He unhooks his pads and lets them drop on the bench. "It's just one game. There'll be other chances to start."

I look over at him and forget whatever I was

going to say. He's got his shirt off now, and his pants too. It looks like they pulled down his boxers a little when he took them off, and now they're hanging off his hips, dipping below the sharp V of his pelvis. I can see a patchy trail of hair running from his navel to the waistband of his boxers, and for some reason my gaze is stuck on it. I follow it down, realize what I'm looking at, and turn my head away quickly.

What the fuck was that? There are tons of naked guys in here, every day, all around me. Half of them have no modesty whatsoever, and walk from the showers to the lockers with their dicks hanging out. But suddenly seeing my friend partially dressed makes my whole body flush, and I don't know if it's from embarrassment or something else.

"We'll keep working at it. I'll make a new schedule to fit around the game."

Griff just grins, shaking his head. "You and your fucking schedules, man."

He closes his locker, and when I glance over at him again, there's a towel wrapped around his hips. It's not hanging as low as his boxers were, thank fuck. But I still have to pull my attention away.

"Gonna hit the showers. Meet you at the Den later?"

"Yeah," I choke out.

As he walks away, I try not to think about the fact that he's going to drop that towel soon.

We win the first game of the season.

We pretty much stomped the shit out of Kentucky, even though that's not exactly hard to do these days. But a win is a win, and all through the next week, everybody's riding high. Including me.

The thrill of the season finally hits me, and it gives me something to really focus on. Something I can grab hold of that isn't as confusing as everything else in my life.

Griff was at the game, warming the bench just in case Matthews had to walk off. I'm pretty sure Matthews was taunting him half the game, but at least he got his job done this time.

I wish it was him running the ball into the goal, or catching it right on the sidelines, but he's been pretty cool about it. Cooler than me, at least.

I worked with him three more times since then, trying to figure out what exactly Coach Garvey wants to see out of him in order let him start. That's not counting all the time we've spent at the gym, at the Den, or at the library.

So far he's kept his promise, and even though I don't really have a lot of homework yet, he's helped me feel like I'm actually retaining something from the hours of lecture I have to sit through every school day.

We were supposed to work together today, but the other guys are flaking out on me. There's a dorm party tonight, and all three of them want to be there to pick up chicks who'd love nothing more than to be seen on a football player's arm.

I should probably go with them, honestly. I spend so much time with Griff these days that people are probably starting to talk. But nobody knows he's gay, and it's not like we're blowing each other or something. I'm helping him with football shit and he's helping me with classical lit.

What could be more straight than that?

Frat parties have never been my thing, anyway, so I'm not about to change now. Besides, I found some clips I want to show Griff, and I tell him to meet me at Kensington Park.

The sun is just starting to set when I get there. Coach has started running two-a-days now, and between a two hour practice in the morning, a full day of classes, and a two hour practice in the afternoon, I'm beat.

But I want to see Griff in a jersey, and there's only one way to make that happen.

I sit on the bench with my laptop, sweating it out in the Florida heat. 7 PM, just about fall, and it's fucking 90° out here. At least, it feels that way. Four and a half years and I'm still not used to it.

I hear Griff walk up and turn my head to face him. He's got his hands in his jean pockets and earbuds in his ears. He must've taken the bus to get here.

"Long time no see," he says.

He looks as tired as I feel, and yet he still manages to smile. I'm pretty sure I've been scowling since three o'clock.

"Take a seat. I've got something to show you."

"Is it porn? Because I don't think the two

moms over there will appreciate it," he says, nodding toward the playground. "Plus, I never told you what I'm into."

It's a joke. His shit-eating grin gives it away. But for some reason it makes me feel... Strange. Not uncomfortable, I guess. Just a little weirded out by the fact that I'm now wondering what kind of porn he *does* like.

"It's just football clips. Sorry to disappoint."

He shrugs, then sits down beside me. "Just as good."

That at least makes me laugh, and some of the tension fades away when I roll my shoulders. I still find myself clearing my throat, though, and feeling like the biggest idiot alive.

Turning the laptop so he can see it, I cue up the footage I downloaded earlier. "Watch what he does right as he's about to get tackled."

The footage is of a running back who plays for the Jets, but it's definitely something we can use. He watches the clip with me, all the way up to the tackle and the call to end the play.

"You see that?"

"He sped up right before he was brought down."

I nod. "You ever listen to the defensive coaches? They're teaching players to tackle through the guy, not to be a solid wall."

"So if I've got some momentum going, I should keep it up?"

"Anybody going in for the tackle might not be ready for it. At best you'll get a few more yards before you're dropped, and at worst you'll be at less risk for injury. It's a way for you to control what happens."

Griff nods. "Could always use more control out there. Might be able to shake this finally and just play like a normal fucking guy."

"Stop being so hard on yourself. If anybody else knew what you've gone through to get here, they wouldn't believe it."

A slow smile spreads across his lips. "Pot, meet kettle."

"Do as I say, not as I do," I say with a smirk. "Come on, get off your ass. We're going to give it a shot."

"The other guys already here?"

I stand up and stretch, trying to remember what I was taught in peewee football when we used to try out multiple positions to see which one would stick. For about two weeks, I was on defense.

That was before they found out how far I could throw.

"They're at some party."

"Oh. Cool."

If I didn't know any better, I'd say he sounds a little nervous. That thought is confirmed when I glance up at him. He looks like a deer caught in the headlights, and I grin.

"Relax. I'll go easy on you."

I stuff my laptop into my bag and leave it on the bench before walking out onto the grass.

Griff follows, and I hold up a hand to stop him. "Start here, and run toward me when I give the signal."

"You want me to do it in slow motion, like the movies?"

I roll my eyes, and don't bother to answer him. If I encourage him to be a smartass, he'll just keep it up. No matter how nice it is to have somebody who isn't constantly up my ass about doing every little thing perfectly.

I get about twenty yards away from him to start with, then lift my hand up in the air to signal. I let him start and get halfway before I even go into motion. Best to take it easy this first time.

When we make contact, Griff hits me pretty fucking hard. He's leading with his shoulder like he does when he's protecting the ball, and I'm down low to get a grip around his waist and tackle him to the ground. It doesn't exactly happen that way, though. I have to struggle to keep hold of him, and he almost shrugs me off. He gets at least five extra yards before I can bring him down, and his momentum ensures he can get up easily.

"That was a pretty weak tackle, man," he jokes.

He offers me a hand up, and I take it. "No shit. Been a long time since I did this. Set up and we'll go again."

We do it a few more times, and I eventually remember what I was told years ago. Each time, I start a little quicker, and run at him with a bit more force. By the third tackle, he can't really shrug me off, and I bring us both to the ground easily. But he's still able to get back to his feet, and that's what counts.

"How'd that feel?"

"Like I'm going to have bruises on top of bruises tomorrow," he says, rubbing his side. "But I can see what you mean. Feels less like I'm being tackled from out of nowhere, and more like something I can control."

I nod. "That's the idea."

He makes a good point, though. I probably should've brought pads to this outing. Coach will have my ass if either of us get injured out here.

"Last one. Really push it this time."

He nods, setting up in the same spot as before. The grass has a little divet where his shoes have dug into the ground.

I take my place a little farther back, and give myself more time to get up to speed. I try to cushion the blow when we meet, to avoid putting either of us at risk, but Griff takes my instruction to heart.

He fucking steamrolls me.

I don't know if I just didn't have enough balance, or if I wasn't throwing enough weight into it, but he runs over me easily. He could've kept going, but I think taking me down takes him by surprise, and instead of shaking me off and moving past me, his leg seems to get stuck between mine, and we both fall to the ground.

At first I think I've made him sprain something. Hell, I'm not sure I haven't. But when he starts to laugh, I realize he's just fine.

I also realize that he's on top of me. Pressed against me, body to body. One of his legs is between mine, and his weight rests atop me.

I've been sacked and tackled. Had linemen

85

flatten me to the ground and refuse to get up before. But this is different.

I can feel every hard contour of Griff's body. The way his well-defined pecs move as he breathes in and out. The sleek lines of his pelvis. The weight and warmth of his thighs. And I even feel his breath, hot against my shoulder as he laughs.

There's a part of me that wants to throw him off, and a part that wants to examine every sensation. I'm used to the way a woman's soft body cradles mind, and this is a lot different. Hard. Firm. There's nothing soft about Derek Griffin.

But for some reason, my own body is starting to heat up. When he stops laughing and looks down at me, my breath catches in my throat. Something passes behind his eyes—an unspoken heat—and my gaze fixates on his lips.

A hint of stubble frames them, but they look soft. Sculpted just like the rest of his face.

He shifts a little, and I'm not sure if it's deliberate or accidental, but his thigh brushed against my crotch, and I can feel my dick twitch in my jeans. Breath rushes from my lungs, and I can't move.

I can't think. I can't do anything but lay there, helpless as my body betrays me. Jesus Christ. My dick is waking up while there's another guy on top of me.

It has to be some sort of weird physical stimulation, right?

Because if it isn't... Then I have a lot more to figure out about my life.

CHAPTER TEN
- Derek -

Shit.

I don't know when it became weird between us, but it's definitely moving into that territory now. I thought Hawk would be laughing right along with me, but when I look down at him, all I see is confusion. Confusion and something else that I don't want to examine too closely.

There's no way this can end in anything but disaster.

I scramble off of him, and mumble an apology under my breath. Swallowing hard, I rub the back of my neck as if I can somehow chase the thoughts out of my head.

I should've gotten off of him ages ago, and if I'd realized I was fully on top of him, chest to chest, hips to hips, thigh to groin, I would've done something sooner.

At least, I hope I would have.

Because my dirty little secret is that in that moment, I wanted nothing more than to kiss him.

Those full lips were so inviting, parted softly in surprise. I wanted to lower my mouth to his and finally taste him just like I've done in my dreams so many times before.

Even now, the thought of it races through my mind. Would he shove me off immediately? Or would he go with it, just to see what it's like?

There's no good answer to that. I know better than to pine after straight guys, but being around Hawk all the time is fucking with my head.

"Hey, I just remembered I've got a paper due tomorrow. You mind if I cut out a little early?"

It's the lamest excuse ever, but Hawk still looks a little shaken up. He's finally pulled himself off the ground, and his clothes are rumpled in that sexy way that definitely isn't helping my hormones.

I wonder if he can see right through me— see into my lustful mind. I fucking hope not.

"Yeah, sure," he says, and his voice is a little strained.

I stand there like an idiot for a moment, as if either of us are suddenly going to say or do something that will change what's become a very awkward situation.

Grabbing my bag from the bench, I head toward the entrance to the park, trying not to think of the feeling of Jason Hawkins beneath me.

Homework definitely doesn't help.

I actually do have a paper due tomorrow, but like the nerd I am, I've already finished it. My roommates are both gone when I get there, so there's nobody I can rely on to fill my mind with stupid shit that has nothing to do with Hawk.

Instead, I'm left to sit at my desk, staring at my laptop and trying not to go with the most obvious means of relief.

Jacking off to images of a straight guy is a slippery slope. Especially when that guy is my friend.

But I can't help it. I feel like a man starved, tempted with the smallest taste of food and desperate for more. My hand seems to act of its own accord, and before I know it my zipper is down and my already half-hard dick is in my hand.

I try to soothe my conscience by surfing to my favorite porn site, but it's not the actors I'm thinking of as I stroke one out.

It doesn't take me long to come. My body's been holding this in for a long ass time, apparently. And as I shudder in post orgasm bliss, I also start to feel that post orgasm shame.

It's not like Hawk is ever going to find out, but now I'm thinking this won't be the last time I have to seek a little relief.

And there's no way I can deal with a whole year of this shit.

After I clean up, I grab my phone and open an app I haven't used in at least a year. I'm not really big on hookups. Casual sex is nice for a quick fix, but I've always wanted something more than that. I'm not a huge fan of fucking some guy I just met who doesn't give a shit about me beyond what I can do for his cock. I'd rather have someone who loves me; who will take care with me and meet me halfway to give us what we both want.

It's stupid and sappy, but it is what it is. Unfortunately, I've put myself between a rock and a hard place with this Hawk situation, and right now, an anonymous fuck is just what I need.

My body's just pissed that I haven't given it any attention in a while. If I can quiet it down, maybe it will stop making me ache for straight guys.

I swipe through the app, looking at pictures of abs and pecs and almost-dick pics. Nobody actually posts their headshot here. It's like a buffet table where you pick out exactly what you're craving most, no strings attached.

I already know what I'm craving, and I'm definitely not going to get it. Best to look for a distant second.

I wish a few of these guys would at least post some pictures of their lips, if not their full faces. It would give me a chance to indulge in fantasy without pushing it too far. But instead I have to settle for body shots, and I try to pick a guy who looks similar to Hawk in physique.

Athletic body. Defined pecs. Strong arms. Taut stomach. A little dusting of hair. Close enough.

The guy could have the personality of a brick and it won't matter. The few times I've hooked up in the past, the bottoms have only had one personality: The desire to be fucked. Right now, that's exactly what I need.

I send a message and fire off a couple more just to make sure I can line something up. In a college town like this, there are always tons of horny gay guys. I'm bound to find something.

And then I can finally get Hawk off my mind.

Of course, it doesn't help when I see his name light up in my notifications. I check my texts and see him ask my help cramming for a psychology test tomorrow once I'm done with my paper.

Not great timing, but I did promise make him a promise. I don't want Hawk to fail because I'm having issues. Now that the semester's started, he's back in a dorm, so I pack up my shit and head over there, hoping it won't be weird.

An hour later, I'm sitting in the one chair he has in his dorm room, his psych book on my lap, trying not to fall asleep.

I love learning about psychology, but this book is so fucking dry that it's no wonder he's having trouble studying for his test.

"I'm never gonna get this," he says, and his fingers curl around the edge of the bed. Something I immediately draw my gaze away from before my brain gets any ideas.

"Probably not from this book."

I snap it closed and toss it aside. It thuds on the floor, as useless as it was open.

"Why don't we try this a different way. You trust me?"

He gives me a strange look, then nods. For the next hour or so, I pull some analogies out of my ass. It's pretty impressive, if I do say so myself. I speak to him like he's a coach, because I think Hawk would make a pretty damn good coach, and because a lot of what coaches do involves psychology.

I give him a couple hypothetical problem kids to work with, and apply the theory he's supposed to be learning for tomorrow's test. It takes him a bit of practice, but seeing it laid out like that makes it click for him.

While he's taking notes, though, my phone chirps. With him occupied, I decide to check it and see a notification from my app.

One of the guys I messaged has gotten back to me already.

Flicking my gaze to Hawk, I make sure he's still busy before I open up the message. I don't know why, but I feel a little guilty looking at this here. As if I'm somehow betraying him.

The text is concise. *Dazzle @ 10 tomorrow.*

Dazzle is the stupidest fucking name for a gay bar I've ever heard, but it's the most popular one in town. And I guess having a name like that keeps the really straight people away.

I text him back, trying to get some details on what he'll be wearing or what he looks like so I can recognize him and not make an ass of myself. As I'm in the middle of it, though, Hawk's voice interrupts me.

"Texting your boyfriend?" His voice is a little rough.

"Hah. Funny. Haven't had one of those since high school. Just a, ah... Hookup. Maybe."

I feel like I've been caught with one hand in the cookie jar. Hawk is looking at me with a mix of surprise and something else I can't read. So much for this not being weird.

CHAPTER ELEVEN
- Jason -

I shouldn't care about Griff texting some guy, but for some reason it puts me on edge.

It's not like I give a shit what he does or who he does it with, but I did ask him over to help, not to sext. He could've turned me down if he had other plans.

The more I think about it, the more I can't focus on taking notes at all. Griff seems to pick up on my agitation, and puts his phone away. Even across the room, I can see it light up again.

"It's cool. Write him back. Not like I don't have shit I can be doing."

"I'm good," he says, and I can feel the weight of his stare even as I look down at my notebook.

He's probably wondering what the fuck crawled up my ass, and I wish I had an answer for him.

We work for a little while longer, but I can tell he's getting frustrated because I don't seem to be making any headway past a certain point. Putting the psych lesson in coaching terms made a big difference, but my brain is choosing to focus on Griff's phone now, and it doesn't help that I can see it light up again every few minutes.

"You should answer. Seems like this guy really wants to talk to you."

"Yeah, well. Desperation isn't a turn on for me." He reaches over and turns off his phone.

It feels like a small victory, but before long

my brain is stuck on the subject again. What's going to happen after he leaves my dorm? Is he going to call this guy? Maybe hook up with him?

And why do I even care?

"This somebody you know from class?"

It takes him a minute to realize what I'm talking about, and I already want to take it back. I don't actually want to have this conversation, but I can't seem to stop.

"Fuck no. At least, I hope not. It's just some guy from an app. I don't even know his name."

A few of the guys on the team use apps like that to get laid. I guess it shouldn't surprise me that the gay community has something similar.

I tried it out once, when I was feeling too horny for my own good. But I didn't really like the anonymity of it. It felt hollow. Worse even than picking somebody up at a club or a bar.

Maybe that's what's wrong with me. I don't want Griff to have to deal with the same kind of shit I dealt with. He deserves a lot better than some random hook up.

"You gonna meet up?"

He looks to me like I've just grown a second head, then shrugs. "Don't know. Probably. He's a good-looking guy, and I haven't been laid in a while."

Those words make my body heat up again, and I suddenly remember having him pressed against me in the park. Fuck. I've tried so hard not to think about it, and I definitely don't want to think about it now.

"You got somewhere in mind?"

"He wants to meet at Dazzle. Not really my first choice, but it's a pretty common place to meet."

Dazzle. It takes me a second to realize what that is, then I remember the few times I've driven past it. It's the largest gay bar in town, situated right between a dance club and a tattoo shop on the downtown strip. Music is always thumping in that place, and every time I've driven past it, I've seen a few guys going in and out.

For some reason, though, the idea of Griff going there doesn't really add up in my mind. It seems like it's beneath them. The whole casual scene, picking up some random guy to take home for the night. But fuck. We're both in college. Isn't that what college guys are supposed to do?

"You want company?"

The words come out before I even realize I've said them. Whatever's making me so agitated has also managed to convince me that it's a good idea to go with Griff to this bar.

And now he's looking at me like I'm fucking insane. He isn't wrong.

"You do know it's a... Gay bar, right?"

I shrug. "Yeah, so?"

Griff arches a brow. "Not exactly your scene."

Now I have to dig myself out of this hole I've created. I could go back on my offer, act like I was just joking. But there's still a part of me that won't budge on it.

"You're my friend," I say as casually as I can manage. "I can still be your wingman even if I'm

97

straight, right?"

"Yeah, sure. I guess."

I have to keep digging. "Plus, you don't know this guy. He could be a serial killer or something."

That actually makes him laugh. An honest guffaw that I can tell catches him off guard. Finally, I'm off the hook.

"A serial killer? Really?"

"It could happen."

We spend the rest of the night arguing about the logistics of a serial killer who preys on random hookups at a gay bar before finally getting back to psychology. I've managed to dodge a bullet here, but I can't help thinking that I've just gotten myself into an even bigger mess.

CHAPTER TWELVE
- Derek -

It feels really weird bringing my straight friend to a gay bar.

Not that there aren't other straight people here acting as wingmen or just enjoying some time out with friends. Despite the glittery façade, Dazzle is a pretty low judgment zone, so a lot of people who don't like regular bars come here because it feels less threatening.

It's pretty easy to spot the gay guys who brought along a straight friend, but I don't see any of them standing too close, or giving lustful looks, so I can't imagine there's anyone else caught up in the same predicament as I am with Hawk.

I should be thinking about the guy I'm here to meet. He actually texted me a picture of his face, and he's pretty good-looking. Not a 10, but neither am I. And he's got a nice body, so that's really all that matters for some random hookup. At least, that's what I'm tell myself.

I almost decided to make up some sudden illness, but Hawk had a bug up his ass to get us here on time. I don't know what's up with him. Ever since I texted this guy, he's been distant and short with me.

He's not making any sense, and the fact that he's so uptight about this is stressing me out. It doesn't help that he walks into the place stiff as a board, afraid to leave my side or even look around.

"Nobody's going to come over here and

molest you just for looking, man. Trust me, you give off the straight vibe loud and clear."

Fuck, now *I'm* getting snippy. This night's definitely not going to end well.

"It's not that," he says in a gruff voice. "I just don't like crowds."

It's a shitty lie. We're packed together like sardines in the locker room, and the halls of Eastshore College aren't much better. But maybe he just doesn't like the bar scene. There's a special kind of claustrophobia that takes place when you're surrounded by drunk people and loud music.

I'm not going to bug him about it. Truth is, I'm thankful for his company. I always feel like a perv doing this alone, and even if it's super weird having Hawk here, at least I have a backup plan if everything goes to shit.

Then again, what if everything goes well? What if this guy asks me back to his place or even just to his car for a quick fuck? Am I really going to be able to walk back to the dorms with Hawk like nothing happened?

"Show me the picture again?"

I fish out my phone and open picture of the guy am supposed to meet, flashing it to Hawk. Because this isn't a weird at all.

"I think that's him over there," he says, nodding toward the bar.

Hawk's right. It's a dead ringer for the guy sitting at the bar, sipping on a martini.

"Last chance to bail," I say, glancing up at my friend.

"I'm good."

I just shrug and start toward the bar, trying to derail my natural instinct to turn right back around and leave. I must be one hell of an introvert, because we've only been here a couple of minutes and already I'm already over this place.

Either that or my treacherous mind is trying to tell me not to waste my time.

I sidle up to him and drop into a bar stool. Hawk stands beside me, his arms crossed over his chest like he's my goddamn personal bodyguard.

"You Tommy?"

Tommy. What kind of self-respecting adult calls himself Tommy?

He turns in his chair, and to his credit, he has a killer pair of blue eyes and a great smile. He looks like the kind of guy who could get away with selling vacuums door to door. "And that'll make you Derek."

His voice is a little higher than I expected, and sitting in front of him, I can see he's wearing eye and lip liner. I don't have anything against guys who are a little more femme, but it's not really my type. Still, it's not like I'm here for a long-term thing. I'm not even going to see much of him when I'm standing behind him later.

I offer my hand, and he shakes it, then his attention turns to Hawk.

"I didn't realize this was a two-for-one deal."

Agitation flares in me, a byproduct of whatever the hell has been building all night. I can feel a sense of possession wanting to creep in and take hold of Hawk as if he belongs to me, but I manage to tamp it down long enough to choke out a reply.

"He's straight," I say, and it comes off as more of a warning than anything else.

Tommy sticks his bottom lip out in a pout. "Sad."

Tell me about it.

"Sorry to disappoint," Hawk says behind me.

"He just came with me to make sure you're not a serial killer or anything." Despite my mood, I can't help but smile a little at that.

Tommy takes it as a smile directed at him, and I know it really should be. If I'm going to do this, I need to give it the old college try.

Tommy and I get to talking, and he actually seems like a pretty nice guy. Whether he picks up on my mood or not, he manages to put me at ease. At first, he tries to include Hawk in our conversations, but I can tell it's making him uncomfortable.

After a few minutes, Hawk excuses himself with the Coke he ordered from the bar and goes over to watch one of the TVs that's currently playing highlights from the UF game.

As soon as he leaves, Tommy kicks up the flirting to 11. He touches me constantly, every time he talks. First on the hand and the arm, which I don't mind so much. Then on the knee and the leg. Finally he goes for the thigh, and I tense.

He backtracks, and it takes me two beers before I loosen up enough to get over my fucking self. I'm the one who asked for this. We both know I'm here for a hookup, so I need to just calm the fuck down.

The next time he does it, I let him. His hand slides over my leg, and he slowly massages my thigh as he asks me about the classes I'm taking. I can feel a familiar twinge in my groin, and I know I'm finally starting to get somewhere when I suddenly see Hawk out of the corner of my eye.

"Have some fucking class, man."

My eyes widen and I just stare at Hawk. He's looking down at my crotch, where Tommy has his hand still firmly planted over my dick.

Hawk steps a little closer as if he intends to pull this guy off of me. What the fuck?

Tommy lifts both of his hands into the air. "Forget it. Not interested in boyfriend baggage." He looks down at me and makes that pouting gesture again. "Pity, too. You're a hot one. You ever want a three-way, you know how to find me."

I just watch Tommy walk away, completely stunned. The music is a distant, droning sound, and everything in the bar just blurs into a world of dark and light.

When I look up at Hawk finally, he's still watching Tommy, his jaw clenched hard enough that I can see the muscle working underneath his skin.

I stare at him, open mouthed, having no idea what to say until he finally turns to look at me.

"What? That guy was a dick."

I can't hold it in. I just go off on him. "What

the fuck is wrong with you?"

He seems genuinely surprised by my response, and his stricken look clenches around my heart.

"He was all over you as soon as I left."

I keep staring at him, hoping he'll get it on his own. When he doesn't say anything else, I shake my head.

"I came here for a hookup. What the fuck did you think was going to happen?"

He looks away from me, holding his head. I don't know what he's feeling right now, but I'm completely overwhelmed by a mix of total shock, agitation, and confusion.

"What would've happened if I hadn't been here? Would you have let that guy fuck you? Maybe let him drag you off to the bathroom or something? Or let him blow you right here in front of everybody?"

I can't even believe what I'm hearing. "You're being a real asshole right now, Jason. What the fuck is your deal?"

He takes a step back from me and looks genuinely distressed. It only takes a moment of that expression to rip my anger away. This fucker has me on one hell of a roller coaster ride. One second I'm pissed at him, and the next I'm feeling sorry for him.

"I don't know. I gotta get out of here."

"Fine." Back to being catty, I guess. "It's not like I asked you to come here, anyway."

He looks up at me, nods, and then turns and bolts for the door, not paying attention to anything around him. As I watch him storm out, I know I can't go through with whatever little indignant hissy fit I'm planning. Swearing under my breath, I toss some cash on the bar to settle our tab, and follow him out to the street.

This time, his long ass legs aren't going to save him. By the time I throw open the doors, he's at the end of the block, hands stuck deep inside his pockets, waiting for the all-clear to cross at the intersection.

I don't even know what I'm going to say once I get up there, but I can't just let him storm off. He was a dick in there, but a part of me is afraid there's something more going on here. There's also a part of me that's afraid I've just thrown our friendship away, even though he's the one sticking his nose into my business.

Fuck. So much for being assertive.

"Hawk! Wait up." He moves across the street at a good clip, and I make it to the curb. "Jason!"

I swear again and follow him across the street, even as the signal changes. Someone lays on their horn. I flip them off, then jog up behind Hawk and eventually step in front of him. He looks away from me immediately.

"Look, I'm sorry. I lost my shit back there. I just need some time alone."

I should just let him be. He's throwing down boundaries, and I don't want to run this any further into the ground. But his behavior is freaking me out.

"Sorry for fucking up your chances," he says

again, the words almost mumbled.

He won't look at me, so, running on instinct, I put my hand on his face. His stubble is rough under my fingers, and I feel a little tingle run through me at just this innocent contact.

Jesus. Not now.

"I don't care about that guy." *I messaged him to get my mind off of you.* "I just want to know what the hell is going on. Are we cool or not?"

He just looks at me, and his blue eyes have this openness about them that I've never really noticed before.

But right now, I have no idea what's going on in his head. There's no way. Because every signal—from the way he leans in close to me, to the way his gaze keeps flicking down to my lips—is telling me he wants to kiss me.

His tongue darts over his lips in the same way it does when he's busy concentrating. Only this time, his focus seems to be on me.

I can't even catch up to the possibility before his mouth comes down on mine.

CHAPTER THIRTEEN
- Jason -

I have no idea what I'm doing.

Kissing another guy? Really? And a guy I'm starting to consider my best friend, to boot?

But I can't stop it. The moment he puts his hand on my face, I'm done for.

I had to get out of that bar because I couldn't stand the thought of Griff going home with some random guy. The feeling that's been bothering me isn't just annoyance at him possibly ditching me. It's jealousy.

All night, I watched them. I watched that asshole Tommy flirting and groping and fucking him with his eyes. I watched Griff respond to it. Watched the way he licked his lips and leaned in closer.

And that's what I ended up focusing on. His lips. I wondered what they would feel like. What they would taste like.

I had to know.

All of these fucking emotions are so pent up inside of me that I just have to get them out somehow. I should've waited until Saturday and just worked my ass off during the game like I always do when I need to forget, but it's already too late for that.

The second my lips press to Griff's, I know it's not just going to be a quick peck. This isn't some kind of test between bros to see if I'm actually interested.

I'm definitely interested.

His lips are softer than I expected, and while he's stiff at first, it doesn't take him long to respond. His mouth melds to mine, and the light scratch of his stubble is a strange new sensation that just seems to heighten the little shocks of pleasure that explode at the end of my nerves.

I don't know how a first kiss between Griff and I should go. It's not like I planned this. But I know what I need, and it isn't soft or gentle.

My lips crash roughly to his. I take his face in my hands, feeling the short, coarse hair beneath my fingers, and use my body to push him backwards.

I don't even know where we are, but when he stops, letting out a puff of breath as his back hits a wall, I take full advantage.

I kiss him in a way I've never kissed anybody before. His mouth opens to me on a moan, and it's the sexiest sound I've ever heard. It's also an invitation. I take it immediately, thrusting my tongue into his mouth and meeting his eagerly. His own hands move down to my chest, and he grips my shirt in his fingers, pulling me even closer.

I kiss him until I can't breathe anymore, and after a gulp of air I go right back to kissing him, pressing my body to his the same way we were pressed together in the park. Only this time, it's deliberate, and the throb in my jeans doesn't surprise me at all.

My body's on fire, and everything in me craves this closeness. I want to somehow be nearer to him, but practically every inch of me is melded to him, his hard body against mine. And the more we kiss, his tongue meeting mine time and time again, my lips crashing against his teeth, the more I can feel him get harder still.

I can feel the bulge against my thigh, and, running on instinct, I adjust myself against him so that he can feel me, too.

He lets out another moan that I swallow greedily, and I work my hands down to the sides of his neck, his shoulders, then eventually to his hips, pulling him closer against me.

The honk of a horn followed closely by a few whistles and slurred, feminine cheers of encouragement rushes over me like a bucket of ice water.

I pull myself away from Griff, and he just stands there—or rather, leans there—his back against the wall, eyes half lidded, lips a little swollen, face flushed.

There's a part of me that just wants to go right back to what we were doing. Desire courses through my body, so hot and so strong that I don't feel fully in control of myself. Slowly—way too slowly—the world around us starts to come back, and I realize we're standing on a street corner, giving everybody a show.

"Jesus," Griff breathes, his chest heaving.

I can't seem to catch my own breath, and it doesn't help when panic begins to set in.

I just kissed another guy. And because I can't seem to do anything half-assed, I didn't just kiss him with the mild curiosity of an experimental college student. I kissed the fuck out of him, like I wanted to devour him right here in public.

A part of me *still* wants that.

I rake a hand through my hair, letting out a heavy breath. I have no idea what to say. What are you supposed to say when you suddenly realize you aren't straight?

Because there's no denying it now. I liked it. Not just my body, though there's no denying that, either. My bulge is huge right now, and my cock is straining painfully against my jeans.

But I enjoyed it on some deeper level, too. Something about it just clicked. Like it's been a long time coming.

It's overwhelming, and even though Griff is staring at me, waiting for an answer he rightfully deserves, I can't give him one.

"Sorry. I don't..."

I haven't stuttered or tripped over my words since I was in grade school. But now my tongue feels heavy in my mouth, and I can't manage to form the words in my brain.

"I... Have to go."

My feet don't want to move. It's like I'm waiting for Griff to say something, do something, but he looks just as surprised as I am, if not more so.

"... Okay. Yeah. I'll... Catch the bus."

I squint my eyes shut as realization hits me. I'm his ride. I can't cock-block him, kiss him, and ditch him all in one night. I have to at least try to not fuck *one* thing up.

"No. Sorry, I... I wasn't thinking. I'll drive you back to your dorm."

I finally start walking, as if my brain has finally decided it's okay with this decision. I can't look back at Griff, and it takes a while, but I eventually hear the sounds of his sneakers hitting the pavement as he follows.

The ride back is more awkward than I could have ever imagined. Neither of us say a word to each other, and I can't even stand to listen to the radio. Instead, I focus on the sound of the wheels moving smoothly over the asphalt, the light squeal of the brakes, and the rhythmic click of the turn signal.

Anything to keep from thinking about the fact that I probably just destroyed our friendship.

CHAPTER FOURTEEN
- Derek -

For the next two weeks, I do everything in my power to avoid spending time alone with Jason Hawkins.

I work my ass off to get my brain right and internalize everything he and the other guys have been teaching me. The last drills I did with Hawk are what have really clinched it for me, though, and I even manage to stand up to Coach Garvey's test of a tackle drill without breaking a sweat.

Go figure. The guy I'm trying to avoid is the one guy I can't get out of my head, even when I'm not thinking about that kiss.

Hawk doesn't look like he's faring much better. Every time I see him, he's focused and determined. Giving his all and then some for football, just like he did when I first met him. It blindsides me a bit, to realize just how much he's loosened up since we started hanging out. And I feel like an asshole for mostly ignoring him, but Hawk doesn't seem eager to strike up a private chat with me, either.

It's better this way. He's confused. Doesn't know what he wants. And he needs some space to figure it out.

I just can't handle being involved with a straight guy who doesn't actually want me, and Hawk has better things to do than worry about whether or not he's jeopardizing our friendship by pursuing his curiosities.

It's not like I'm never going to talk to him

again. Right now, I'm hoping we can make it through this semester, then just kind of reconnect as friends once this blows over. Is it naive? Fuck yeah. But I don't know what else to do.

A part of me really wants to confront him. Ask him point blank what he wants. Ask him if there's anything between us, because that kiss... Jesus. I've never been kissed like that before. Hawk kissed me like he actually wanted me. Like I was the only thing in the world that mattered at that moment.

But I know it's not true. Either my mind is playing tricks on me and I'm remembering it way better than it was, or... I don't know. I just know there's no way Hawk could ever be as into me as I'm into him.

It doesn't look like our little separation is going to last through the semester, though. As I grab my bag from my locker, I see Hawk coming up to me.

He looks cool, collected, and confident, but when I meet his gaze, I can see uncertainty in his eyes. I just want to stroke his cheek and tell him it's all going to be okay, but I keep my hands to myself and try to act casual.

"What's up?"

"Hey. I know you've got your own shit going on, but are you free tomorrow night?"

My heart thumps in my chest, and a little tremor of anticipation snakes through me. "Yeah, I'm free."

"I've been trying to write this Western Civ paper all week, and I wouldn't mind having a second pair of eyes on it."

I deflate quicker than a terrible Patriots joke. What exactly did I think he was going to do? Ask me out in the middle of the locker room?

"Yeah, I can take a look at it. You want to email it to me, or...?"

He reaches up, and I watch the pads of his fingers scratch over his stubble. I can't help the memory that surfaces. I know exactly what it feels like, and I practically ache to touch him again.

"That's cool. Unless you feel like coming over. I wouldn't mind going over it in person."

I hold his gaze for a moment, and try to figure out if there's a double meaning there. He doesn't cave, but I can see a bit of a plea in his eyes. Maybe he's as tired of the separation as I am. Maybe it's time we both get past our drama and figure shit out.

"Sure. I'll bring a pizza or something. We'll work it out."

He claps me on the shoulder, and even that touch—the same touch I get from teammates every day—is enough to send my heart racing and set my body on fire.

So much for giving him time to figure things out.

I get to his dorm room around seven o'clock with a large pizza tucked under my arm. It isn't the first time I've been here, but this time, it feels different. Something crackles in the air, just

117

waiting to ignite, and I'm equal parts giddy and terrified.

In the few hours since practice ended, I've come up with a plan. I need to know where we stand. Even if he tells me it was a one time thing—some crazy, spur of the moment reaction—I need to know. It's driving me crazy to wonder.

I hear Hawk's voice when I knock, and he opens the door soon after. He's dressed in a Tigers t-shirt with athletic shorts, and I get a pretty generous view of his muscular arms and legs. I'm reminded of just how ripped he is for a quarterback, and already my thoughts scurry to a place they shouldn't.

Unlike me, Hawk doesn't actually share a dorm room with anybody else. He had a roommate at the beginning of the year, apparently, but they transferred and he's managed to fly under the radar ever since. Now, a month into the semester, I'm not sure anybody's going to join him. Fine by me, because I don't like the idea of having this conversation knowing somebody could walk in on us.

"Hey. Thanks for coming over."

"No problem," I say, setting the pizza down on a little storage unit since he's got his laptop set up on the desk.

I open up the box, and the smell of greasy cheese, pepperoni, and sausage hits my nose. Coach Garvey gets onto us about eating fast food, but we put in enough work during the day that a few slices of pizza aren't going to kill us.

We both eat and talk about the upcoming

game. We're four games into the season, and I still haven't been called on to start yet. I'm trying not to freak out about it, but it's honestly starting to get to a point where I know I'm going to have to consider financial aid.

"What are you going to do if you can't get a scholarship at the end of this year?" He asks after taking another bite of pizza.

Talking with him like this makes me realize how much I missed having my best friend around.

"March my ass down of the financial aid office, I guess."

"Nothing to be ashamed of. Most of the people who attend this college aren't doing it out of pocket."

I nod, but it doesn't really make me feel any better. My parents tapped out their savings paying for my medical bills, so I can't ask them for help. But they also lectured me about getting buried underneath a mountain of student debt.

It's not like I have a wealth of options right now, though.

"Do you qualify for any academic scholarships? You still have a 3.9 GPA, right?"

"Yeah, me and at least 70% of the student body. Most of the scholarships are for high school seniors, anyway."

"Guess I'm part of the 30%, then," he says.

I start to feel like an asshole for even saying it, but when I meet his gaze, I can see a small grin tugging at his lips. I smile in return, and feel a little bit of my tension ease.

That is until we lapse into silence while we

eat, and my mind spins with what I actually want to talk to him about.

Drawing in a deep breath, I try to salvage what's left of my courage and man the fuck up. "We have to talk about what happened."

He doesn't respond for the longest time, and just silently chews the bite he's taken before washing it down with a Coke. His posture is insanely rigid, and I'm not even sure how he can manage the movement to reach for another slice of pizza.

"Don't want to," he finally says.

I'd say neither do I, but that'd be a lie. "Didn't take you for somebody who runs from his problems."

He sighs, tossing the slice of pizza back into the box. "I don't know what you want me to say, Derek."

His tone is defensive, and my hackles immediately raise. Great. This is how it always ends with straight guys.

Instead of talking about it and admitting he might be feeling something he doesn't want to feel, he's just going to bury it and act like it never happened. Wonderful.

Wiping my hand on my jeans, I stand up and start toward the door. "You can just email me the paper. I got shit to do that doesn't involve feeling like an asshole for something you did."

Before I can even reach the door, his hand is on my arm. His grip is desperate, and I can't help but look at him. He's fixing me with the same pleading blue eyes that got me here in the first place.

"Wait." I stop moving, and take my hand away from the door, letting out an agitated sigh. "I'm sorry. I'm just... Confused."

"Join the club," I mutter.

He takes his hand off of me, and I immediately feel the absence of warmth. So fucking pathetic. I can't even make a stand for myself without pining for him.

"How did you figure out you were gay?"

The question isn't completely unexpected, but I have to bite back the first smartass answer that comes to mind. He's trying, at least.

I draw one arm loosely about myself, as if it's going to protect me from getting hurt here. "It's just something I always sort of knew. Ever since I was a kid, really. I just liked being around boys more than girls, and eventually that turned into something else." With a sigh, I give in, sinking back into the chair. Hawk moves to sit on the bed. "In junior high, I went on my first date with a girl. She kissed me, and I didn't feel anything. I dated girls through my sophomore year of high school, and it was the same thing every time. The first time I kissed a guy, I felt... Amazing. Like I was finally doing what I was supposed to do."

He looks out the window, and I join him. A couple of skinny guys are tossing around a football. When I look back at Hawk, he's got both hands behind his neck, and he's hanging his head down like he's this close to puking. Jesus. And I thought it was hard for me to come to terms with my sexuality.

But that's putting the cart before the horse. I'm bracing myself for him to tell me he didn't really feel anything; that he was just horny as hell and I served the same purpose any warm body would.

"I've never felt anything for another guy. Never even thought about it until I met Nathan. I guess I started to wonder my senior year of high school. What it would be like if we fooled around, you know? He was my best friend, and I figured my life would be pretty fucking perfect if I was gay, because we already got along."

I give him a small smile. I can empathize. "I get it."

An ache burrows its way into my chest. For years, I've done everything in my power to keep from thinking about Danny. Somehow, now that I'm desperately trying to avoid wanting another teammate, it keeps coming up. Go figure.

"Never had the balls to talk to him about it, and after a few months away from him at college, I didn't feel that way anymore. Didn't wonder about any of the other guys. Until you."

He lifts his gaze and captures mine. There's such a vulnerability in his eyes that I'm struck speechless. Once I realize I'm waiting for him to say something, though, I force some air back into my lungs and get over it quick.

"Straight up, no bullshit: Did you like kissing me?"

My heart hammers in my chest as I wait for his answer. I can practically hear the blood whooshing in my ears, drowning out everything else.

"Come on, man. I'm pretty sure you felt the answer to that."

I laugh, and a little of the tension eases out of me before coiling right back up like a spring. "I know your dick liked it. Did *you* like it?"

He takes a minute to answer, looking everywhere but straight at me. I forget how to breathe, and my chest starts to burn. This is going to kill me. I'm going to be wheeled out of his dorm on a gurney, brought in DOA to the nearest hospital. Cause of death: Wanting a straight guy.

"I don't know, Derek. I think so."

I let out a breath and try to tamp down my excitement. 'I think so' isn't really an enthusiastic 'yeah, man, let's totally fuck.' But it's better than flat-out denial.

"But how's that even possible? I haven't been faking it with girls."

Nothing against Hawk's old girlfriends, but I so don't want to hear this.

"It's called being bi, dude. Playing for both teams."

I'm not surprised he thinks it's all or nothing. Most gay guys I know think that, so I figure it's the same for straight guys, too.

"Shit." He leans back in his chair, and I watch as he stretches his arms over his head. His muscles flex, and I feel a familiar warmth in the pit of my stomach. "So... What now?"

Now you get rid of your clothes and let me lick every single inch of that body, I think, and my dick twitches in agreement.

I almost wish I had the balls to say it.

"That's up to you. If you want somebody to... practice on. You know, just to make sure you really feel that way. I could probably help."

Jesus. Because that's so much better? I can't believe I just said that.

He leans forward on the edge of the bed, clasps his hands together, fidgets a little. Then he seems to realize what I said, because he looks up at me and a slow grin spreads across his lips. "Probably?"

I couldn't bite back the smile even if I tried. "Yeah. I guess I could work something out. Have to check my schedule."

He laughs, shaking his head, and the sound is like music to my ears. "You're a dick."

"Yep."

As I listen to him, I can feel the tension flow out of the room. I feel like I'm sitting with my friend again, instead of someone I can't figure out. But when he looks at me, those blue eyes practically twinkling with amusement, a whole different kind of tension passes between us.

Swallowing hard, I stand up from my chair and cross the short distance between us. I stand in front of him, and my stomach is already doing flips, my nerves wrecked as I think about what's coming next. One kiss is no big deal. We could probably get past that and write it off as a fluke. But kissing in his room? On his bed?

Things are going to change between us, and maybe not for the better. But I still can't keep myself from sitting beside him.

CHAPTER FIFTEEN
- Jason -

When I feel Griff's weight push down into the bed, I know things are about to change. It's like staring up at the sky right before a storm comes through.

"Looks like my schedule's pretty clear now," he says, and his voice has a roughness to it that blazes a trail of anticipation straight through me.

I see Griff's adam's apple bob as he swallows, and feel a weird burst of nerves flutter through me. It's like I'm a teenager again. Sitting alone with someone in my room. Wanting to kiss them, knowing they want it, too, but scared to fuck it up. Everything in my life has always had to be perfect, and I feel like my previous experience isn't really going to count for much here.

My gaze moves down to his lips, and I see his tongue flick across them. I remember what it felt like in my mouth, against my own tongue, and for the first time I let myself wonder what it would feel like somewhere else. Against my nipples, maybe. They've always been sensitive. Or my cock, which is already starting to firm up in my jeans just at the thought of getting some action from Griff.

I moisten my own lips, and realize he's waiting for me to make the first move. So I screw up my courage, lift my hand to rest on the side of his neck, and meet his lips with mine.

He expects it this time, so there's no awkward moment of him being stiff. He meets me halfway, and his eagerness stokes the fire that's quickly growing in me. When his tongue swipes across my lip, I open for him and let him take the lead, enjoying the feeling as he strokes mine with a slow, exploratory touch.

The longer we kiss, the more vocal he gets. It starts off as soft, barely audible sounds that are more vibrations against my mouth than anything else. As my tongue tangles with his and my hands begin to explore the hard planes of his body, the sounds get louder and longer. Low, masculine moans that send liquid heat straight to my groin. Fuck, that's sexy as hell.

I touch him over his clothes, tracing over his shoulder muscles, his arms, then inward over his collarbone, his pecs, and down to his abdomen. I can't really touch too much more than that, and I let out a soft groan of frustration against his mouth.

"We can always get more comfortable, if you want," he says, and demonstrates by lying back on the bed.

I look down at him, splayed out before me. His shirt's come up a little bit, revealing a stretch of his tight abdomen. I can see the light patch of brown hair that dips just beneath the waistband of his jeans, and my dick seems to appreciate the sight.

With him laid out before me, his arms behind his head, it's an invitation to touch wherever and however I want. I draw my tongue over my lips, my mouth suddenly feeling dry as a desert.

"Scoot all the way onto the bed," I say softly, my voice a little deeper than it usually is.

He obeys, moving until almost all of him is draped over my bed. He doesn't completely fit, and he has to draw up his knees a little bit, but all of him is laid out before me now, begging to be touched.

I take full advantage, feeling a curiosity and excitement I haven't felt in years. I start with his face, enjoying the rough scratch of his stubble beneath my fingers. Then I moved down to his throat, and leave my hand there for a moment as he swallows beneath me.

I move down, over his chest, finding his nipples through his clothes. My thumbs brush over them and he shivers, closing his eyes. A satisfied grin spreads across my lips as I realize he's at least as sensitive as I am, if not more. It's something I want to explore later, but for now, I've set a goal for myself. A limitation: Over the clothes action only.

Honestly, if we do much more than this, I'm a little afraid I'm going to start thinking with my dick instead of my actual brain.

For now, though, I'm content to touch him as is. And because that little bit of skin is showing, I consider it fair game and run my fingers over his abdomen. The hair there is soft against my skin, and a part of me wants to rub my cheek against it. It feels weird to even think that, but I guess desire always makes you think strange things.

That and the fact that, as soon as I touch him, skin to skin, his muscles flinch underneath me, and he sucks in a breath.

"You're going to do this until you have me begging, aren't you?"

My grin broadens. It's not my plan, but it is appealing.

I move down, using both hands to follow his thighs. He's got the legs of a runner, thick and muscular and just begging to be touched. It's amazing to me that one person's body can feel so different from another's, but where I'm used to soft, supple flesh beneath the fabric, Griff gives me hard, defined muscles that seem to tremble at my every touch.

I move my hands a little inward, and my gaze fixes on the bulge in the front of his pants. I hear him hiss as I get close enough to tease him, but not close enough to give him any relief.

I know this is going to be a turning point. For some reason, in my head, all of this is okay. It's just a little bit of experimentation. But when I touch him in a more intimate way, it means something else. It means I'm committing to this. That I actually want to be with him. To please him and have him please me.

Fuck it. I can't take it anymore, and I'm dying to know what he feels like. Even through his pants.

I expect it to be like cupping myself, and it mostly is. He's warm against my hand, and I can feel the outline of his shaft through the fabric. He's already rock hard, and my pulse quickens as I realize that's all because of me.

But the biggest difference between touching

him and touching myself is that I get to enjoy his reactions. One of his hands goes to his forehead, and he looks up at the ceiling, muttering something under his breath. It sounds like a plea, and as I rub him through his jeans, I watch his every reaction. His lips part, his hips arch off the bed a little, and his chest starts to rise and fall rapidly as his breathing becomes more ragged.

"You're kinda killing me over here," he says, and his voice is raspy, playing on my already excited nerves.

"You want to even the score?"

I want to keep touching him, but I have a strong need to slide my hands under his shirt, and I know if I do that, it's not going to be long before his clothes come off. It's not really a bad thing, but since I've set this arbitrary goal for myself, I want to stick to it.

Of course, Griff doesn't know about this goal, and he can do whatever he damn well pleases. When he motions for me to lie back beside him, I do it, looking over at him as anticipation tangles within me. I'm already so wound up that, as soon as he touches me, I can feel my dick throb in my shorts.

That's when I realize he doesn't even have to get me out of my clothes to be able to reach more of my skin. My shirt sleeves are short, and he has full access to my arms. He takes advantage of it, tracing the definition there in an almost reverent way.

He does the same thing with my chest, and down to my abs. Then he dips his hand underneath the hem of my shirt, and smooths it up over the front of my body.

He rubs in slow circles, and my breath hitches as he gets close to one of my nipples. Even just the slightest touch from him makes me let out a moan that doesn't sound like me. I arch into him, and let my head fall back against the bed.

"You like that?"

He does it some more, the soft pads of his fingers running over the flats of my nipples. They stand stiff and taut, pressing hard against my shirt, and with every pass he makes, the tension in me winds tighter and tighter.

I should have told him the rules, but I can't say I mind that he's indulging a little. When he draws away from my chest, it takes everything in me to hold back the most pathetic whimper ever. But he quickly makes up for it, running both of his large hands down my thighs, and coming up underneath the hem of my shorts.

I'm wearing boxer briefs underneath, thank God, because I don't think I could take the feeling of him touching my inner thigh, skin to skin. Even this is almost too much, and my dick starts to beg for attention. When I look down at Griff, he's looking right back at me, his eyes blazing with need.

I don't know who leans in first, but our lips meet in a searing kiss. I crush my mouth to his, moaning against him as he gets closer and closer to where I want him.

Finally, he rubs me through my briefs, and I almost come right then and there.

"Fuck," I hiss against his mouth.

He keeps his lips less than an inch from mine, and I can feel his hot breath against me as he focuses on what he's doing. The movements of his hand are slow torture, and he rubs with his palm, eventually using his fingers to trace the outline of my shaft.

Dipping his hand between my thighs, he cups my balls and squeezes a little, and I arch my hips up off the bed to get closer to him. The last time I was touched like this, I was a teenager, and I'd never been touched in any sexual way before. It made sense that I couldn't control myself back then, but now, years later, I feel like I'm about to have the exact same experience.

When he starts to stroke me in earnest, his fingers closing around my cock, I just can't help it. The tension in me explodes, and before I realize it's happening, he's bringing me one of the most intense orgasms of my life.

He stops touching me directly as it happens, and I clutch at his shoulders, my fingers digging into his back through his shirt. I can't manage the brainpower to focus on kissing him, so instead I bury my head against his shoulder, his fingers tangling in my hair.

His other hand gently caresses my thigh, and my muscles jump and twitch as I reach the point of oversensitivity.

I let out a shuddering breath, and the reality of what just happened hits me hard. My cheeks flush, and for a minute, I can't really look at him.

132

"Shit. Sorry. I haven't done that since high school."

I'm not a teenager anymore. I should be able to keep it together and not come in my jeans. Griff's probably regretting being my mentor right about now.

Way to completely kill the buzz, self.

But he just puts a finger to my mouth, then replaces it with his lips. It's a slow, sensual kiss, and unlike the last few, neither of us seem to be in a rush.

I let myself relax against the bed and enjoy his mouth on mine, and when he finally breaks the kiss, I feel a little more at ease.

"Don't be sorry. That was sexy as fuck."

His words are a huge surprise to me, and I feel a swell of emotion in my chest. "Yeah?"

He kisses me again, smiling against my lips. "Yeah."

Now I want to make him feel good, too, and I decide it's probably time to go back on my rule. I won't take off his clothes, but I want to actually feel him this time.

I slide my hands over his chest and up to his shoulders, pushing him gently so I can change our position. He lays back on the bed, and I move on top of him, enjoying the feeling of his body against mine.

It's still almost too much stimulation when our hips meet, but I tough it out, and decide to experiment a little. I roll my hips against his, and he tilts his head back, reaching one hand behind him and gripping the edge of the bed. He moans, and I drag my lips over his jaw and down to his neck, finding the frantic beat of his heart beneath my mouth.

When it's too much for me, I slide my hand over his thigh, and search out the button of his jeans. My other hand joins the first, and I undo his fly.

"You sure about this?" He asks, and he's practically panting already.

"I'm sure."

I cup him through his boxers first, and he gives in to me completely, one of his hands digging into my shoulder, the other gripping the sheets.

I reach in and stroke my fingers along his length. He's already rock hard, and the velvety smooth skin feels amazing. I decide to go for it completely, and pull him out of his boxers, venturing a glance down.

He's bigger than I expected, and the sight of his cock standing to attention, hot and hard against my palm, makes me ache in a way I've never felt before. I start to think about all the things I could do to him, and my curiosity rises as I wonder what he'll taste like.

And what he might feel like inside of me.

I know I'm not ready for those things yet, and I know Griff won't push me. For now, I just want to give him the same pleasure he gave me. Looking up at him, I meet his gaze. It's fucking intoxicating to see his half lidded eyes glazed over with lust.

I squeeze the base of his shaft, then run my finger over the sensitive slit, just like I do with my own dick. It's amazing being able to rely on a bank a pre-existing knowledge, even though I know there's bound to be differences between us. It's like I have a foundation to draw from, and I'm not just going into this completely blind.

Or worse: Schooled only by the Internet.

As I slowly stroke him, I learn that Griff really likes it when I apply a little more pressure right underneath the head. He also likes it when I rub the pad of my thumb over that sensitive skin just beneath, and when I trace the seam of his balls.

He prefers a pretty tight hold, and moans more and more as I jack him. I watch his face the whole time, loving his reactions, and loving that I'm able to do this for him. I keep up a vigorous rhythm, my motions slicked by his leaking slit, and it isn't long before he starts lifting his hips off the bed, thrusting up into my hand.

The sounds he makes when he's close to the edge are about to make me hard again, and when I see and hear him tense, a moan catching in his throat, it's the most exhilarating feeling in the world.

He comes hard, and I stroke him through it, keeping my hand around the lower part of his shaft to avoid the sensitive head.

He shivers a little as he comes down, and puts both hands over his forehead, running his fingers through his hair and letting out a breathy laugh.

"You sure you haven't done this before? That was fucking amazing."

Pride swells in me, and when he leans up to kiss me, I meet him eagerly. A part of me is still ready to go again, but I know we should probably take a little break and actually finish that paper I asked him over here to look at.

Neither of us have to say anything. I flop back on the bed beside him, my hands on my chest, feeling calm and satisfied for the first time in weeks, if not months. It's like something in my life has finally clicked in the place, and I didn't even know that piece was missing.

Griff takes a little catnap beside me, and I don't even notice until I see the rhythmic rise and fall of his chest. I watch him sleep, and a strange sensation flutters through my chest.

I'm not sure what all will happen between us, or what we've just started. But I feel like I've started something that's going to change my life.

CHAPTER SIXTEEN
- Derek -

Two weeks later, Hawk and I have continued our marathon make-out sessions.

Most of the time, they take place in his dorm room. It's just safer that way, since there's no risk of anybody walking in. But when I know both my roommates are out, I bring him over to my place, we play a couple games of Madden, and then fool around for an hour or so until we both give into the fact that we have other shit we need to be doing.

As far as I'm concerned, it's the perfect life.

We haven't really moved beyond handjobs yet, but that's totally okay with me. Watching Hawk jack me, feeling his hand around my cock, it's absolutely mind-blowing. Better than anything I've experienced before, from getting a blowjob to fucking.

I'm not going to pressure him for more, but when we get there, I know it's going to completely ruin me for any other guys.

Thankfully, the fact that we spent so much time together before this means the guys pretty much know what to expect from us. It's not weird when we leave the Den together, or when we spend a lot of time hanging out and talking in the locker room, like we are today.

But when Coach Garvey asks to see me in his office, the first thing I think is that we've been found out.

Hawk seems to think that, too, because he

looks at me with surprise and a little bit of apprehension.

"You schedule a meeting with Coach?"

"Nope. This is news to me."

I give him a smile that I hope is reassuring, but as I make the short walk to Coach Garvey's office, I can't help but feel my own nerves kick in. Right now I'm pretty much getting to have my cake and eat it, too. It's like living in a dream, and I'm just waiting to be snapped awake at any moment.

If Coach knows about us—and if the other guys find out—that's it. Things will change. Hawk will probably go back to acting straight, and I'll be stuck as the lone gay guy on the team. Again.

I know it's unfair even as I think it, but considering my past, it's hard not to.

By the time I get into Coach Garvey's office, I've already got a chip on my shoulder. I pull the door closed behind me a little harder than necessary, and Coach looks up, one white brow raised high.

"Somebody piss in your Cheerios this morning, son?"

"Just didn't get a lot of sleep last night, Coach," I lie.

He nods toward one of the two chairs in front of his desk. "Have a seat, Griffin."

I do as I'm told, trying not to fidget as I wait for him to just spit it out. He has his reading glasses on, and he's looking at some paperwork. The top seems to be stamped with some kind of letterhead from a lab, and I wonder if it has anything to do with why he's brought me in here.

"Reiner won't be playing in Saturday's game. Do you think you'll be able to get enough sleep between now and then?"

He looks at me over the rims of his glasses, and I just stare back at him, a little baffled. Whatever he's getting at, I'm not really following. So Reiner isn't starting? What does that have to do with me?

"Don't worry, Coach. I'll be fresh for practice. It won't affect my game."

"Good," he says, and I hear the swish of his pen tip as he signs a piece of paper.

We sit there in silence for a minute, and I wonder if he's trying to sweat me out like this is some kind of interrogation. Coach was a big help to me when I first came to Eastshore, but maybe he's decided I've just been wasting his time this year. Maybe I haven't made the progress he hoped.

"Make sure you don't overwork yourself at practice. I want you starting on Saturday."

He says it so offhandedly that it takes a moment for the words to words sink in. I play them on a loop in my brain, and at first they just jumble into a mess that doesn't make any sense. When they finally click, I can feel my mouth open, and I see the corners of Coach Garvey's turn up just a little bit.

Cheeky bastard.

"Thanks, Coach," I say, trying to hold in the gushing.

I don't want to end up being the 'aw shucks, do you really mean it' kind of kid who doesn't realize his own worth to the team. Then again, I've questioned it lately. I've worked my ass off at practice, but without the chance to play in a real game, I've felt like a serious third wheel when Hawk and I have hung out with some of the other starters.

"Don't thank me. You worked for it. Good job, Griffin. I expect to see the same hustle on the field."

We're scheduled to play another school that's just hit Division-I status, and an out-of-conference school, at that, so I know this is a trial run. But I'm thankful to have it.

I wait in the chair, buzzing with energy, until Coach waves me off.

"That's all. Get out of here. And don't drink too much. I expect you here for practice, five o'clock sharp."

"You got it, Coach."

He knows us too well, and I'm suddenly glad he isn't one of those hardasses who doesn't let his players have a little fun during the season. The Tigers Den would see a lot less business, for one, and it's a harder to celebrate such a huge thing when you're sipping on a Coke Zero or something.

I let myself out of Coach Garvey's office and Hawk is standing on the other side of the door. An image of him with his ear pressed against it flicks through my mind, and I have to hold in a laugh.

"Everything okay?"

Do I fuck with him? I think I have to fuck with him a little bit. I decide to keep my voice somber, like I'm trying to force the emotion out of it because I'm afraid of me teammates seeing me disappointed or, God forbid, sad.

"Yeah. No big deal."

I walk out into the locker room, and Mills, Carter, and West are waiting, too. They try to cover it up and act like they were just hanging by Hawk's locker, but all three of them look up when I come back.

"Oh, cool. You're all here," I say, and I'm this close to losing it already. I'm such a terrible liar. "I wanted to say thanks for helping me out this season."

"Shit," Mills says, tossing his balled up jersey into the bottom of his locker.

I can't watch this anymore. Hawk looks like someone kicked his puppy, and the other guys are about one step away from marching into Coach's office and telling him what for.

"...Because I'm officially starting on Saturday."

"No fuckin' way!" West jumps up from the bench, throws an arm around my shoulders, and yanks me into him hard enough to bruise.

"You guys free? Drinks are on me tonight."

"You bet your ass they are," Mills says, moving in to clap me on the shoulder.

The guys congratulate me and give me shit about not pissing my pants in the game Saturday, but the whole time, I can't take my eyes off Hawk. He looks... proud. Almost bursting with it. I've never seen that look in his eyes before, and it means more to me even than the chance to start.

Knowing I've done something to please him

makes everything that much more worth it.

We get to the Den around seven. Pretty early for the regular crowd, so we have our pick of tables. It's the five of us, plus another couple guys who tagged along. I offer to buy their drinks, too, and get a couple pitchers sent over to our table, along with a couple baskets of hot wings.

Once the beer starts flowing, the guys get a little crazy. Dante and Carter are always super competitive when they drink, and just an hour into it, they've roped everybody else into an argument about whether or not SCU's penalty was justified all those years ago.

I don't really have a horse in the race, so I give up pretty quick. Besides, I'm more focused on Hawk, who sits right beside me. Close enough that I can touch his thigh with mine, and I do it pretty frequently. The first time he jumped a little, but he's slowly gotten used to it, despite giving me a very weak 'knock it off' look.

Normally I wouldn't be so aggressive in a public place, but with a little buzz and some amazing news, I'm feeling great. So as the other guys are deep in their argument and at least three glasses down each, I decide to kick it up a notch.

I slide my hand under the table casually when no one's looking, and run my fingers along the outside seam of Hawk's jeans. His knee bumps against the table, and I grin.

He looks at me, and I slowly slide my hand

143

over his thigh. I can see the heat in his gaze, along with the warning, but he has two working hands. If he wants to stop me, he can. Since I feel no resistance whatsoever from him—and he even moves his thighs a little further apart—I continue with my plan.

I check to make sure the guys are still talking about whatever the hell they're talking about. Mills is flailing his arms about the way he does when he gets really drunk and really opinionated. West looks close to climbing over the table and punching him in the face. None of them are even remotely paying attention to anything else.

And then there's Hawk. Poor, unsuspecting Hawk, just sipping his beer. I grin as I realize he's probably going to have a little trouble concentrating on that soon.

My hand moves further inward, just brushing over his crotch. I feel the muscles in his thigh jump, and see him look at me out of the corner of his eye. My grin broadens, and I pretend to look at the TV, just to keep up the facade.

Thursday Night Football is on, but I couldn't tell you who's playing. All my focus is on Hawk as I do everything in my power to make him as hot for me as I am for him. I want to blow this place and blow him, and I'm only going to get that if I can get him to want me.

I squeeze lightly. He isn't hard yet, but he isn't completely soft, either, and I know it won't take much work for me to get him where I want him. I flick my gaze back to him and see him swallow down a gulp of beer, and I run my fingers over his bulge.

I keep it up for a good five or ten minutes, rubbing slowly as he comes to life beneath my hand. At one point, it looks like he has to bite his lip to keep from moaning. I just grin like the cat who ate the fucking canary. I know I'm getting to him, and it isn't much longer before he caves.

"Bored with you assholes. I'm going home." His voice is so strained, and I look over at the guys to see if they've noticed.

But only Carter even realizes Hawk said anything. "Your loss, dude."

"Probably not," I hear him mutter thickly under his breath, and I bite my own lip. "Stand in front of me when we walk out."

He says it in the same tone of voice, just loud enough for me to hear, and I grin. "What? Am I your boner shield now?"

"You cause it, you take the fall for it."

"Gladly," I say, putting my hands above the table again and taking one last drink like I haven't been rubbing another guy's dick under the table.

"Hawk's my ride. I'm out, too."

A few distracted, slurred 'later's and 'congrats again's come from the guys, and I pay for my shit before taking up my post as certified boner guard. Hawk walks close to me, acting like he's just keeping track of me in the now-thick crowd, but I know he's trying to get me back for the game I played earlier. I can feel his breath tickling the back of my neck, and it's driving me crazy.

As soon as we get outside, I look for

someplace we can go. But the downtown strip is pretty busy, filled with pedestrians and drivers. And there's no way I'm going anywhere near one of these alleys. So I tug him toward the parking garage, figuring it's the safest—and closest—place we can be.

He didn't bring his car. We both knew we'd be drinking more than a few beers tonight, and it's not that long of a walk to the dorms. But I just can't wait. I pull him into the elevator with me and look for a security camera. There's one outside, but not inside.

Feeling half-starved, I shove Hawk against the wall so hard the elevator rocks a little. He's not even surprised. Instead, he meets me step for step, his lips crushing to mine in a fiery kiss. We're a flurry of lips and teeth and tongue, and I can't seem to get close enough to him, pressing my whole body to his, grinding my hips like a needy whore.

When I pull back, he looks drunk, and not just from the beer.

"Think I can make you come before the elevator hits the top floor?"

"No," he rasps out, but I'm already unzipping his pants.

"Give me a head start and make sure that door stays closed."

"That's cheating," he says, but moves over to the side of the elevator closest to the buttons, finger poised over 'close elevator.'

"You're the one about to get blown here. You really care if I play fair?"

146

He lets out a husky laugh, and I start to hate the fact that he wears boxer briefs. He told me he likes the support, especially playing football. But it's fucking inconvenient for blowing him in public. What an inconsiderate asshole, right? I smirk as I tug his pants and underwear past his hips, watching his cock bob free.

My boy's already hard for me. I might actually win this bet after all.

CHAPTER SEVENTEEN
- Jason -

I can't believe we're doing this.

Maybe it's the beer or the high of knowing Griff's going to start on Saturday. Maybe it's just the fact that feeling his hand on my dick the whole time we were in the Den made horny as hell. But right now I don't care that we're in a very public elevator; that we could be caught at any moment, arrested and probably put on probation.

Right now, I just want him, and whatever he's willing to give.

His words are hazy in my mind, but when his knees hit the metal floor of the elevator, rocking it again, I realize what he said. *You're the one about to get blown here.* Oh, fuck. Griff's going to suck me off in an elevator. Right here, right now.

The doors start to open, and I slap my palm over the button, closing them as quickly as I can. We're hidden from immediate view, but that isn't going to stop somebody from seeing us if they mash the button on the outside.

My heart races, but all of my anxiety fades away the moment his hand closes around the base of my cock. He jerks me hard, just the way I like. My impulse is to moan, but he claps his hand over my mouth before I can get the sound out. Right. Public elevator.

It's a good thing he did it, too, because when his tongue traces the length of me from base to tip and back again, I can't control myself. My moan is muffled against his hand, my hips buck forward, and the elevator rocks for the third time.

"Easy, cowboy," he says with a throaty chuckle.

Easy for him to say.

He repeats that same stroke a few more times, runs his tongue around the crown of my cock, and I suddenly wish we were still on the back wall so I could hold onto the railing. When he flicks against the slit and then presses firmly to the underside of the head, I damn near lose it.

He may win this bet after all.

The elevator threatens to open again, and I slam my fist into the button. It's a lot to concentrate on at once, and when he finally swallows my cock, I'm not sure how useful I'm going to be as a lookout.

My head thumps back against the metal panel and I moan against Griff's palm. He presses his lips firmly against my skin, sliding down and back up with a crazy amount of suction, letting up only to use his tongue at the best possible moments.

It's fucking amazing.

It's not like I haven't had a blowjob before, but there's something different about this one. Maybe it's because Griff's a guy. Maybe it's because he's really good and I'm really into it. But he seems to know exactly what I want. He gives attention to the sensitive spots, keeps a good pace, and doesn't have some irrational fear that he's going to break me somehow.

He even gives attention to my balls, first

150

with his hands and then with his tongue, running along the seam, laving each of them in turn before drawing them into his mouth and sucking. Fuck, that almost does me in, and my hips buck.

I'm so close to coming. Just the right flick of his tongue is going to be enough to push me over the edge.

But then I hear the clicking of heels outside, and some of my high evaporates, replaced by ice cold dread. "Shit. Head start's over."

I slam the button for the fourth floor, the highest possible in this parking garage. Knowing he's lost me a little bit, Griff redoubles his efforts. He works me like a pro, and it's not long before adrenaline and the thrill of almost being caught crash against pent-up desire.

Release comes over me in an explosive burst, and I cry out, barely muffled by his hand. He loosens his lips and backs off the head, but he keeps himself right there, swallowing everything I give him.

I'm panting and soaring and so far detached from reality, but it's still the hottest thing I've ever seen.

He grins up at me, looking damn pleased with himself. My legs feel like jelly and I want to bask in the glow of post-orgasm bliss, but the elevator door dings, signaling we've reached the fourth floor. Griff pulls my underwear and pants back up, zips me, and moves to my side, stuffing his hands into his pockets and whistling.

A woman waits on the other side, and my heart catches in my throat. Fuck. Did she hear us?

But when she says something, I realize she's on her phone. My eyes close in relief, and I step off of the elevator with Griff. Once it closes on her and goes down a floor, I let out a laugh that's practically giddy from the flood of adrenaline still pumping through my veins.

"You're fucking insane."

"Yep," he says with a glowing smile that brings out his dimples. "And you owe me fifty bucks."

I shake my head, starting toward the stairwell on shaky legs. No way we're taking the elevator again. I'm going to get hard just thinking about it.

"You never made a wager."

"Well shit." He follows me into the stairwell, and his voice bounces a little on the bare walls. He really has lost his mind.

Apparently I'm right there with him, because I find myself saying, "I'll make one now, though. You help me win on Saturday, I'll blow you, too."

I look over my shoulder at him, and his eyes almost seem to glitter in the harsh fluorescent light. "Deal."

Man. I already wanted to win that game, but now I have one hell of an incentive.

CHAPTER EIGHTEEN
- Derek -

When Saturday rolls around, I feel absolutely unstoppable.

At least... I do after spending most of the morning feeling like I'm going to hurl.

Around 9AM, I got a text from my teenage sister, Grace, that started off with the phrase 'Yo, loser' and ended with 'I'm blowing off Trevor to watch you juggle your balls. Don't choke.'

Grace and I have practically made a career out of giving each other shit. While anyone else would read that text and wonder if my sister even likes me, I know exactly what it means. She's proud of her big brother. And she'll never let me live it down if I'm intercepted today.

That makes me feel a little better, until I get a text later from my mom saying she and Dad had both taken the day off to watch me play from home. I knew they'd been keeping up with the Tigers—they'd sent me texts every week, both when the games were broadcast and when they weren't. My dad especially likes to analyze everything and tries to give me some "inside information" about how I might be able to best one of the starting players.

But them getting the chance to see part of my elbow during a bench shot is a lot different than them seeing me play. My parents haven't watched me since my last day playing football in high school, and considering what a fucking disaster that was, I guess I can give myself a little break for feeling so much anxiety.

I didn't even know this game was going to be broadcast anywhere outside of someone deciding to illegally record it on their phone or something. As a newly-minted Division-I school, Eastshore doesn't get a ton of attention. Our rivals for today, Raleigh Tech, get even less.

But nope. Apparently our game is a feature on one of the ESPN channels. I don't know who our athletic administrators had to blow for that to happen, but it's just one more added bit of pressure.

All morning I consider telling Coach Garvey to give my starting position to someone else. I'm afraid of choking. Afraid all my work with Hawk and the other guys won't really pay off—that I'll see the defender coming at me and freeze up. Drop like a stone where I stand. Or worse, drop the ball completely.

But then Hawk comes up to me and personally hands me my jersey. It's in pristine condition, and even has that new jersey smell that I love so much. It's a bold, deep blue with black accents. Griffin is printed on the back above my number, 22, in blocky white letters for everyone to see.

It's ridiculous to say a piece of clothing changed my mind, but in a way, it did. It was a symbol. Just like that old mesh practice jersey that I'd now stained with my blood, sweat, and tears, this brand new jersey was an indication of just how far I'd come.

"You're going to kick ass today," Hawk said

to me, giving me a smile that made my chest clench. And then he winked, and I felt a whole other sensation. "Don't forget our wager."

How could I? It's all I thought about from that night in the elevator up until this morning, when I instead started to stress about the game. But now that he's brought it up again—no pun intended—my mind is focused on that prize.

Maybe it's a little pathetic that I'm more motivated by the idea of seeing Hawk on his knees in front of me than I am by the idea of not making an ass of myself on national television, but it gets me going and gets me out of my own head.

By the time I hit the field and line up with the other guys for the national anthem, I'm fucking pumped.

I stand a few feet away from Hawk, but it feels like I'm right there with him, my helmet clutched in one hand, the other over my heart as one of the Eastshore students belts out the familiar lyrics. When she's done, we get ready for the toss, and Hawk—now the offensive team captain, just like he deserves—calls it in the air.

We get possession first, and the moment Hawk's fingers touch the laces, I can tell we're going to dominate.

It helps that I'm pretty much thrown into the fire from the word go. The first time he pitches me the ball in a short screen pass, I have guys all over me. Three of them pin me to the ground less than a second after completion. I don't know if Hawk did it deliberately to break me in, but it snaps through that mental barrier and gets me thinking I can actually do this—I can outrun the guys covering me, pick the passes out of the air before they even leap for them, and outrun them on the way to the endzone.

The first time that actually happens, I'm fucking ecstatic. The NCAA has a sportsmanship clause now, so I can't celebrate the way I want to, but damned if I'm not spiking the fuck out of that ball in my head. When Hawk rushes up behind me and lifts me off the ground, it's the greatest feeling in the world.

But not everything can be perfect. Even in a game we're favored to win with overwhelmingly positive odds.

The Rams have a strong offense, even if their defense is a little weak. They get the ball down the field and manage to keep pace with us pretty well. The gap, at its largest, is only seven points. They can close it with an unanswered TD and come out on top with a two-point conversion.

We go into the locker room up by just three, and Coach Garvey gives us a lecture about not getting cocky. We were in the same position as these guys just a few years ago, after all, and it's clear they want to prove themselves in Division-I ball just as much as we do.

Maybe more than we do, because the third period starts with a clusterfuck. Mayes fumbles. One of the linemen recovers, but we're pushed to fourth down and end up having to punt it away. Our defense holds up this time, and the clock runs on and on with no one managing to complete a drive.

Hawk is getting frustrated. He always hurries up to the line of scrimmage when his patience is thin, and while he's normally calm and cool under pressure, I can tell this game is starting to get to him.

About ten minutes into the fourth quarter, Raleigh Tech scores.

Everybody on the Eastshore sidelines is having a fit. The fans are loud and rowdy and I can't even hear myself think as Coach Garvey pulls Hawk off to the side, grabs his face mask to bring him closer, and tells him something. A play, I'd guess, because when we take the field again after special teams clears it, he jogs up with me and tells me what's going on.

"I'm going to call a Slant, but I want you to run it like a Hook. Just head for the sideline and sprint. I'll get the ball to you."

I nod, realizing I trust him implicitly. It's a hell of a pass to make, and a hell of a chance to take on me. The clock's ticking down, and we've got only a few chances at possession to make this work. If Hawk wastes one of them on a play that might not come together—a play that hinges on me not losing my shit—we may end up going home with another one in the loss column because of me.

But it's his call. If he thinks I can do this, then I'm going to do everything in my power to live up to it, because I know he can throw the pass.

He barks out the play, his voice rough from having to shout over the last couple hours. My pulse races, and I make the mistake of locking eyes with the defender standing across from me. When I move in the backfield to change up position the way Hawk calls it, he moves with me. There's murder in his eyes, and a self-satisfied smirk I can just barely see behind his mask.

As soon as Hawk takes the snap, I sprint toward the sideline. I move faster than the guy covering me expects, and he lags behind at first. But when I can't sustain the speed, he gets a chance to catch up, and he's on me practically bound for bound.

But at least he's the only one. We're so far down the field that nobody else would bother coming out here.

I see the ball sail through the air, thrown high and strong. It's moving past me, I can tell, and I have to put on another burst of speed to get to it. The defender is still right there with me, ready to interfere. When I jump for it, his arm comes down between mine, trying to bat the ball away.

But I pull it out of the air and clutch it to my chest.

The crowd roars when they realize I've caught the pass and I'm already at the 10. The defender roars, too, but in a way that says I'm about to get the shit pounded out of me. From the 3 I leap, and so does he. He tackles me around the middle, and I go for the risky move—I stick the ball out with my right hand, holding onto the thing for dear life.

I crash to the ground hard, my helmet jostling against the turf, my ears ringing. My vision swims a little and I get the wind knocked out of me. After a moment, I finally manage to look and see where my hand ended up.

The nose of the football is just passing into the paint. The ref signals a touchdown.

The sound in the stadium is absolutely insane. People are cheering, stomping in the stands, I think there are cups flying onto the field. It's the craziest thing I've ever heard or seen, and somehow it's eclipsed by my teammates coming up and damn near knocking me to the ground again once I finally get up.

"That was fucking amazing!"

"Awesome catch!"

"Holy shit, that was insane, man!"

I'm jostled around, my helmet is smacked and patted, my pads get the same treatment, and through it all adrenaline is pumping and I'm invincible. And when my eyes find Hawk, it only gets better. He's more collected than the other guys this time, but the smile and the gleam in his eyes are just for me.

I feel like I've actually made a difference. Like I actually matter. To the team, yeah. Probably even to the fans right now. I can hear "Griffin" being chanted in the stands. But seeing that look of pride in Hawk's eyes is the best reward I can ever think of.

We win the game 21 to 14.

After that last touchdown, the other team

wasn't able to answer, and our guys were running off the sheer exhilaration of it. I swear that feeling can give you superpowers, or at least an untouchable level of confidence. When our offense took the field again, it was clear the defense was shaken. They covered my ass with double the defenders, and though we made a good run of it, we weren't able to score again before time ran down.

Hawk ended up taking a knee toward the end to run down the clock, and we came away with a huge win.

In the locker room, Coach Garvey handed me the ball. Hours later, and I've got it at the Den. The guys are buying me drinks, and I feel like a goddamn hero. And all that for managing to catch a pass. It's amazing, and it only gets better when Hawk nudges my shoulder at one point and, when the other guys are busy carrying on again, reminds me about our wager.

We don't get back to his dorm room until late. This time, I don't goad him and try to sneak him out. Post-game celebrations are always a big deal, and we both wanted to be there for this one. But as soon as we get back to McKinley Hall, my mind is fixed solely on one thing: Feeling Hawk's lips wrapped around my cock.

Once the door is closed, he pushes me back against it and kisses me like he's been waiting to do that all day. His hands are all over me, and I reach around him to squeeze his firm ass, pulling his groin into mine. He grinds against me and I feel the hard ridge of his erection rub against mine, earning a needy moan from me.

He starts to unzip my pants, though, and I stop him.

I'm panting, my heart is about to beat straight out of my chest, and my dick is already throbbing for attention. But I know this is a big step for a guy who, until just a couple weeks ago, thought he was perfectly straight. It's one thing to jack off with another guy and even have your dick sucked by another guy. It's another thing to have that guy's dick in your mouth.

It's not like college guys haven't experimented before. I'm sure there's a lot of curious blowing going on, even in these halls. But for me, it means more than that. I want Hawk to do this because it's something he's into. Not because he feels like he needs to pay me back for blowing him.

Because frankly, I could probably suck him endlessly and never demand anything in return. Just the sound of his moans and the way his body reacts to every little flick of my tongue is enough.

"You don't have to do this if you're uncomfortable with it," I say breathily. "It's really okay."

Hawk stops, his fingers on the buttons of my jeans. He removes them, and for a moment I think he's going to take the out I've offered. I can't help but feel a little twinge of disappointment. Mostly that's coming from my dick, though.

But instead of giving me a smile and going back to kissing me, Hawk just stares at me intensely. His eyes always seem to get just a little darker when he's flushed with desire, and today is no exception.

"Shut up and take off your pants," he says, right against my lips, in the sexiest voice I've ever heard.

I shiver from it, feeling a new rush of heat light up my whole body. "I like it when you're bossy."

I do as he commands, and the clinking of my belt is the only sound as my pants drop to the floor, pooling around my ankles.

"Boxers, too."

My fingers hook into the waistband and I pull them down, letting my fully hard cock spring free. I realize this is the first time he's actually seen all of me. At least in this way, without my lower body being partially covered still by clothes.

I can't feel self-conscious, though, because Hawk is looking at me like he wants to devour me.

"Go sit on the bed."

I follow his command again, stepping out of my clothes. I can feel his eyes on me, and I give myself a little stroke on the way over there, mostly for his benefit. When I sit on the edge of the bed, he comes over to me with just a few short steps, and lowers himself to his knees.

His hands rest on my thighs, and I watch him, rapt, as he sizes up my cock. With just the slightest, testing touch of his tongue, I'm already lost.

CHAPTER NINETEEN
- Jason -

My confidence is a little bit of an act.

It always has been, from school to football to my personal life and everything inbetween. It's the only way I can get through things, because I'm constantly second-guessing myself. Thanks to advice from my dad early on, I've definitely come to live the phrase "Fake it 'til you make it."

He probably never thought I'd end up applying it to this, though.

Griff's body is intimidating. He's made up of hard muscles and lines that flow into one another, pointing me toward my destination.

I've seen him before, and I know how he feels in my hand. But now his size is almost a little overwhelming. I think about the porn I've seen, and I wonder if it's actually as easy to suck a big cock as some of the actors make it look. I also wonder a whole bunch of other things I shouldn't be thinking about, like whether or not he'll taste good to me, or what to do when he comes.

It isn't until I draw in a breath of him that my mind settles. Or, I guess it's probably more realistic to say I just blank out. That scent of light musk totally turns me on, rich and heady and *male*. It pushes all the thoughts and worries out of my mind, and I'm left only with desire.

Desire to taste him. Desire to please him.

Leaning in, I part my lips and push my tongue out, touching it to his shaft. I stroke upward from the base, toward the tip, the same way he did to me. At that first contact, he sucks in a breath, and I know I'm at least on the right track.

His skin is velvety smooth against my tongue, and his taste just reinforces the jolt that's running through my senses as I explore him. I make it to the tip of his cock and start back down, getting acquainted with every inch of him.

He likes a lot of the same things I do. When I move my tongue underneath the head, his hands grip hard into the sheets, and I can feel his body start to tighten a little. He's already fighting against release, and I haven't even gotten a chance to take him into my mouth yet.

I decide to do something about that, and engulf him with my lips. I suck just the head first, and it takes me a few tries to adjust the pressure to the point where I can suck him vigorously without having to worry about teeth.

Once I get there, Griff is gone. He starts to thrust against my mouth, and I let him, wrapping my hand around the base of his cock just to help control him a little so he doesn't push it too deep.

He fucks my mouth, uses me until he's moaning nonstop, and it's sexy as hell. I never thought I'd enjoy something like this, and as he thrusts into me, it makes me wonder what he would feel like elsewhere.

It's the first time I've really thought about being fucked by another guy—by Griff—but judging from my own moans around his cock and the fact that my dick is rock hard in my jeans, I think it's safe to say the idea is more appealing than I thought it would be.

As I let Griff fuck my mouth, I rub myself through my pants, and I can feel when he's getting too close to hold on any longer.

"Fuck, you're gonna make me come," he says breathlessly, his voice almost a growl.

I don't move away, and he takes that as the all-clear. He buries his hands in my hair, and he slows his movements, letting me finish him with my lips and tongue. His release hits fast and hard, and I catch just the slightest taste of him as he pumps into me.

Most of my attention is focused on his groans, though, because he sounds absolutely amazing when he's coming. And to know I'm the one to draw that sound from him? It almost feels better than winning the game today.

"That was amazing," he says, his voice a little shaky, and his praise strokes something inside of me I didn't know needed stroking.

He pulls me up for a kiss, and I can't help it: I'm greedy. I want more. I'm craving something, and I'm starting to realize what it is, but I don't really know how to ask for it, or even demand it.

Griff takes over and maneuvers me back onto the bed, and before I can think about it, he has my pants and underwear yanked off and he's returning the favor. I close my eyes and let him work his magic, and once we're both spent, I lay there, trying to bring my breathing back to normal while he takes a little cat nap.

I want more of this. I've never been all that sex-crazed before—I've always had too much other shit on my mind—but with Griff, it's like I can't get

167

enough. He's a drug, and I'm the guy who can't quit buying. Can't quit using.

But I'm starting to feel like there's a little more to it than that. Like we're more than just friends who like to get off together. I want him to do things to me I've never even thought about before.

I think I'm starting to have feelings for my best friend.

CHAPTER TWENTY
- Derek -

Hawk and I have spent almost every night together over the past few weeks, and it's been absolutely amazing.

Sometimes we had legit reasons, like when I was trying to prepare him for another test in his psychology class, and then help him figure out the topic of his term paper. Other times we were just hanging out, playing video games or watching football or whatever.

But most of the time we ended up fooling around before the night was through, and I can't say I wasn't always thinking about it in one way or another. I'm twenty-one years old. My cock perks up at the slightest mention of Hawk. So when I have access to him, it's hard to keep my hands off.

Fortunately, he doesn't seem to mind. We spend hours on his bed, kissing and touching like we're both in our teens again and we've never done this before. I know it's mostly true for him, but for me it's pretty mind-blowing. It's not like I don't know my way around a man's body. But with Hawk, everything feels new. I want to commit every line, every little dip, every inch of skin to memory so I can play back the images in my mind when we're apart and feel him on my fingertips, taste him on my lips again.

It's... intense. More intense than I expected, but I can't seem to take a step back to catch my breath. I don't really want to. Hawk—Jason—gave me his trust. He's asking me to guide him, and I have to jump in head first.

It's more than just the physical, though. Sure, I remember the heat of his body and the way it feels against mine. I remember just how he shudders as he climaxes in my hand or my mouth. I remember the way he looks up at me when he's pleasing me.

But I also remember his sometimes shy smiles. The way he laughs at my stupid jokes. Our not-very-heated arguments about NFL players. How he licks his lips when he's concentrating on homework.

He's my friend, first and foremost. My best friend. It's easy to admit that now. But it's starting to become almost painful not to see him. On the nights when we each have too much shit going on to get together—even just to hang out—I don't feel right. I wake up feeling disoriented and less certain about the world around me.

It's like Hawk is my anchor, and without him, I'm just sort of drifting.

I don't really know how to tell him that, or if I even should. The season is ramping up fast, and we're racking up enough wins to actually start really thinking about post-season. I know Hawk wants to be the top seed and get to the Citrus Bowl, and we're actually on track for it. Ranked #4 in the country, #2 in our division, we're the team that, according to all the sportscasters, "Came out of nowhere and may have a real chance at a national title."

A lot of it hinges on our next game against Tennessee. They're sitting high at the top spot in the SEC right now, but not by a huge margin. If we bump them off in this game, we've got a real shot of pulling ahead.

So I can't really think about what I may or may not feel for Hawk, or what he may or may not feel for me. I have to focus on the game, and I know he feels the same. He's been laser-focused at practice, settling back into the groove he was in when I first met him. Only this time, he seems a little more willing to compromise. He's examining his own play just as much as always, but not analyzing everybody else's. For once, he's actually leaving that to Coach Garvey.

Meanwhile, I'm trying to step it up. When Coach tells me I'll be starting the game, I'm equal parts pumped and fucking terrified, because I know letting the guys down this time is going to count for a lot more than it would have in my first starting game.

On Friday night, we fly up to Knoxville. The airport is only a little bigger than the one back home, and it takes a puddle-jumper from Charlotte to get there. By the time we drag ourselves to the hotel, everybody's pretty much ready to fall into bed. We've been practicing all week, it seems like, and Coach had us reviewing footage of the Vols while we were on the plane, so none of us got any shut-eye.

I'm rooming with Hawk, by some miracle, and it's a blessing and a curse because as soon as we set down our bags and I look at him across the room, my dick—who never seems to get tired—reminds me that we're alone here. Mostly.

Sure, the walls are paper thin, but how often are we going to have this chance on the road?

I can tell he's thinking the same thing, but when he flops onto the bed, my whole body seems to tell me that's exactly what we need. I change into clothes that don't smell like an airport and climb into bed with him. It's just a twin, so we barely fit. My ass is hanging off the side and I'm pretty sure parts of him are hanging off the other side.

But he doesn't tell me to move. In fact, he seems to relax more, pulling me closer. A now-familiar tightness fills my chest, and I rest my head against him.

"You nervous about the game?" I ask.

"Hell yes." His voice is a soft rumble that I can almost feel vibrate through him. I smile as the sensation tickles my cheek. "Coach had me watching hours of footage of the Vols' defensive line grinding QBs into dust."

I laugh. "Yeah, he had me watching receivers making friends with the ground. Motivating."

It was, in a way. I know better than to let myself get outmatched, for one. One of their guys is especially handsy, and will likely try to grab the ball from me. In this game, I know it's going to be better to focus on fundamentals and not try any of the fancy shit we got away with in the past.

But I'm still nervous, and hearing that Hawk is, too, makes me feel a little better.

As it turns out, Coach Garvey's scare tactics are really fucking effective.

Either that, or everybody else on the team can taste the chance for an amazing season as much as Hawk and I. Everybody's on point, and while it isn't the world's most exciting game in terms of trick plays or turnovers or really putting up big points, we manage to outplay Tennessee.

It's good, by the numbers ball-playing. I didn't even manage to score, but I don't care. When we go back to the locker room after the final whistle blows, I feel like that tentative sense of excitement has grown into confident energy. All the guys around me aren't just wondering if we have a shot now. They're sure we do.

So is the press, apparently, because it takes hours for us to be released back to our hotel. The game was an upset in our conference, and the sportscasters are all over it. So much so that Coach Garvey ends up calling a press conference in one of the hotel's larger rooms, and a bunch of us have to sit through an hour and a half of questions about our season, our past, and our potential future.

By the time Hawk and I get back to our room, the adrenaline high of winning the game is pretty much tapped out and replaced by fatigue. We showered in the locker room, so we both just sort of slump into our own beds and fall into a deep sleep.

When I wake up, it's to a slight weight on top of me, and something soft and wet and warm against my jaw.

My eyes open and my vision focuses enough to see Hawk. I can feel his breath, the pressure of his lips, and finally realize he's kissing me. Marking a trail along my jaw. I make a soft sound of pleasure, still half-asleep, and he stops for a moment.

Not exactly what I wanted that sound to encourage.

"Couldn't sleep," he says before he goes back to it, kissing my neck.

His hand moves down my body, and the rest of me starts to wake up before my mind really gets with the program.

"What time is it?" I ask groggily. Because I'm an idiot, apparently. What does it matter what time it is? Hawk is on top of me.

"Around three."

I groan, and not in pleasure. We barely conked out an hour ago. No wonder I'm dragging. Or at least, my brain is dragging. My dick is already starting to respond to the indirect attention.

"Been thinking about it all week," he says, and he runs his teeth over my earlobe in that way he knows drives me crazy.

I shudder predictably, helpless to do anything but let him have his way with me. Not that it's a terrible way to go.

"'Bout what," I murmur, my English skills not so great when I'm half asleep, apparently. "Molesting me in my sleep?"

I'm lucky I manage to crack an eye open long enough to catch his grin. It makes me smile.

"How do you know I haven't already done that?"

I laugh softly. "Good point. Knock it off, though. I want to be awake for the good stuff."

"That's what I'm trying to do now."

His lips skim down my bare chest, and I gasp when his tongue flicks over my nipple. Damn him. I'm stuck between that painful place of really wanting to go back to sleep, and really wanting to get off, and it only gets worse when his hand starts to move down my thigh.

I'm only wearing boxers, so he has an unfair amount of access. He uses it fully, slipping his hand under the loose leg and palming me skin to skin.

"Jesus," I manage, lifting my hips against him. "Okay, you made your point."

I get my hand in his hair and tug him up to meet me, waking up a little more when we kiss. It's still a little slow and languid, and I feel like I'm stumbling a little, but as my body starts to heat up, my mind starts to work right, too.

"Derek," he says after breaking the kiss. He's started using my first name more now, but it still sends a little thrill through me every time, "I want you to fuck me."

Holy shit. That wakes me up.

For a long minute I just stare at him, and he stares back at me. He's waiting for me to say something. Do something. And like an idiot I'm not doing either of those things.

"Are you sure?" I manage to croak out, my throat suddenly scratchy.

Jesus. I'm going to make him not want me before I even get the chance to suit up.

"Been sure for a while," he says, then kisses me again.

Holy shit.

Jason Hawkins wants me to fuck him.

When we started this—and even when I fantasized about it—I always imagined he'd top. I've only bottomed a couple times in my life. Mostly because the guys I've met always seemed to prefer the role, and since I enjoy either, I just ended up topping more often than not.

But I never figured Hawk would be the kind of guy who would be into getting fucked, or even curious about it. He's huge. Bigger than me, built with endless muscle and definitely not what someone would imagine the stereotypical bottom to look like.

Then again, there's nothing stereotypical about either of us, and if Jason really wants to be fucked—even just once to know what it's like—I'm definitely not going to deny him.

He kisses a path down my body, and I know exactly what he's going for before he gets there. My breath still catches in my throat when he takes my cock in his mouth and sucks me hard, though, and my fingers tighten in his hair.

There's nothing slow or experimental about it this time. He has a goal in mind, and that's getting me hard and ready to roll as quickly as possible. He does a good job of it, too. Between his expert sucking and my own thoughts, I firm up quickly.

As if realizing that, Jason pushes himself up. He's straddling my hips, and I run my hands over his thighs as he pulls his shirt off. I watch his muscles flex in the dim light, and groan when he gets off of me to pull down his boxer briefs, too.

By the time I lose my own boxers, he's on top of me again, and his dick rubs against mine. I moan wantonly, dropping my head back. He covers my lips with his, and we grind together until my dick is aching and my mind is filled with the intense desire to be inside of him.

Jason must feel it, too, because as he moves his hips against mine again he asks, breathlessly, "Got any condoms with you?"

"In my bag," I manage, and the words trail right into a pained groan as he gets up to grab them.

Fuck me for dropping my bag right by the door instead of within reaching distance. But it does give me a chance to clear my head just a little bit. Instead of being totally consumed by lust and playing by the whims of my dick, I'm able to think about what we're doing here.

"Grab the lube in there, too."

When he comes back, I can see a little bit of

apprehension in his eyes. That beautiful blue is still glazed over by lust, but he can't hide his nerves from me, and I'm glad for it.

I sit up, then gesture for him to sit beside me. He hands me the lube and a condom he tore off from a strip, but I just hold them both in my hand.

"You ever used any toys or anything? Or just your finger?"

"Finger once, yeah, just to see what it would feel like."

I grin a little. "What did it feel like?"

"Like I didn't know what the fuck I was doing."

I laugh, then give him a quick kiss. "Lie back."

If we're going to do this, we're going to do it right.

CHAPTER TWENTY-ONE
- Jason -

I do as he says, and my heart starts to hammer. As much as I want this, I'm a little nervous, too. Fucking around on my own is way different than actually letting another guy stick his finger inside of me, and worlds away from having him fuck me.

But this is something I want. I have to try it at least once, just to see if I like it. Worst case, I'll hate it and Griff and I will figure something else out. I trust him to take it easy and to give me some time if I need him to slow down or stop.

And it's that thought that ultimately sets me at ease as he climbs beside me on the bed and lays on his side. With my hands folded on my chest, I watch him lube up one finger, and then a second one. My brow arches, and he chuckles.

"Just in case." He kisses me again, and I can feel his smile on my lips. "Bend one of your knees a little bit."

"Feels like I'm at the doctor," I joke.

He smacks my chest lightly. "Asshole. See if I try to make it comfortable for you again."

I expect him to start prodding at places I've never had anyone else prod, but instead he starts kissing me again. It's slow and lacking the urgency of our usual kisses, and I realize he's trying to relax me. His other hand runs up and down my body, and he even grasps my cock and gives me a few slow strokes.

I relax back into the bed, and once he seems

satisfied, I feel his other hand drift downward. He cups my balls and I shudder, then feel him skim along the sensitive skin leading to my hole.

He takes it easy with me, pressing in a little bit at a time. At first it feels exactly the way it did when I did it on my own. A little painful, and a lot weird. He whispers soothingly, telling me to relax, and I focus on breathing as he pushes in deeper.

With the lube and the fact that I'm not clenching, it isn't too bad, it's just a pressure I'm not used to feeling. He slides in deeper, and it's like his finger is at least three times bigger than I remember it. How I'm going to take his cock, I have no idea.

But I know if I let myself worry about this, it's never going to happen. So I try not to think about it, and focus on his lips instead. He still tastes a little like the drinks we had last night, and I remember the high of winning that game. It helps me relax even more, to the point where I can barely feel the pressure.

And then, suddenly, I feel something else. A burst of pleasure that explodes within me.

"Holy shit," I say, my voice shaky.

Derek just grins, apparently not feeling like he needs to explain what just happened. I guess he's going to demonstrate, instead, because I can feel his finger inside of me, stroking something, and it's the most amazing feeling I've ever had.

I don't even know how to describe it. It's a deeper pleasure than getting a blowjob or even fucking someone. Maybe it's just because it's more intimate, but I know if he keeps this up, I'm not going to last very long. Already I'm writhing and moaning against him, pressing my ass against his hand, encouraging him to do more.

When he slips in the second finger, stretching me a little wider, I shudder. The discomfort is quickly replaced by an intense pleasure as the digit finger joints the first.

I devolve into a mess of swears and pleas, until Derek slowly pulls out of me.

I groan, immediately feeling the loss, but when I hear him rip open the condom packet, my body seems to realize that it's going to get exactly what it wants.

"We'll go slow, okay?"

"If you can manage to do whatever you just did again, I don't care how fast you go."

He chuckles, and I watch him roll the condom over his cock. He lubes it up, then applies some of the lube to me, as well. His fingers return, and so do my moans, my back pressing into the bed.

The next time he removes them, he gets into place between my legs, and I can feel the tip of him pressing against me. I hold my breath on reflex, then remember to let it out.

His hand moves up to my chest and he caresses me in slow circles. My heart squeezes as our eyes meet, and I rest my hand against his wrist, holding him to me. Something passes between us in that moment, and I can tell he feels it, too. When he pushes inside of me, he does it so slowly, so carefully at first. I'm grateful for that, because his cock is way bigger than his fingers, and I need time to adjust.

Once my body relaxes, though, I have to shift my hips forward a little to get him to move more.

I feel him, inch by inch inside of me, and it's fucking incredible. When he starts to move and his dick rubs against that sensitive spot within me, I almost lose it completely. I clutch his arm hard, while my other hand grips the sheets.

"Oh, fuck, Derek," I moan as he slowly pushes in and out of me.

"Feels good?"

"Feels amazing."

I run my hand up his arm, feeling the soft hair underneath my fingertips. Gripping his shoulder, my fingers curl against his skin. I pull him toward me and he leans close enough for me to kiss him. It's needy and a little distracted as he continues to move inside of me, and I settle for just having his lips near mine, breathing in his gasps and grunts and groans.

"Harder," I beg, and he finally starts moving in earnest. "Need more."

"Anything you want, baby," he murmurs against my lips.

I've never been a fan of endearments. Especially endearments like that. But coming from Derek as he's fucking me, it sounds like the sexiest thing I've ever heard, and I moan softly as he hits just the right spot.

My legs hook around him, my heels against his ass, pulling him to me. He lowers himself above me, and instead of hard, fast strokes, I can feel every inch of him as he moves deep inside of me. My hands clutch at his back, and by the time he works up a rhythm in that position, I know my nails are digging into his skin.

Every roll of his hips brings a new burst of pleasure until every sensation melds together into almost painful anticipation. My muscles tighten, and as my moans start to get louder, Derek muffles them with his mouth. Right. We're still in a hotel, surrounded on both sides by guys who think we're straight.

Right now, though, I don't care about anything except the way he feels inside of me. As the tension builds, I just let it happen, surrendering completely to Derek. I keep a tight leash on everything else in my life, but here, I know I can trust him. I know he's going to give us both what we want, and then some.

I let him take me to the edge, and with one more thrust, he shoves me over it. I come harder than I ever have in my life, and Derek adjusts his position to watch me, his arms moving to hold my thighs in place.

"Fuck, Jason. You're gonna make me come."

I want that, even if I can't find the words to say it. Even as my mind and body are still reeling, I want to give him the same pleasure he's given me. I don't know if I do it intentionally or just as an after-effect of climax, but my muscles clench around him, and I hear the very start of a moan, loud and low, escape from him before he bites it back.

His movements slow, and finally he stills, panting above me. When he pulls out, it feels like losing some part of myself. I already know I'm completely fucked. Not by the fact that I'm so obviously into guys that there's no mistaking it for anything else, but because I'm lying here, after the best sex of my life, thinking about how intimate it felt. How close I felt to Derek when he was inside of me.

How much I want him to stay in bed with me and push the day back just a little further.

Compared to those feelings, the realization that I'm 100% bi seems really small. Just another new thing I've learned about myself. My dad always used to say you never really find out who you are until you're in your 20's, and I guess it's true.

As I feel my heartrate slow and my breathing gradually return to normal, I wonder what my dad will think about all of this. It was weird seeing him between semesters and not telling him. He and I never talked about a lot of shit beyond football, but this is a major thing.

I should be freaking out about the idea of telling him; of telling everyone. Now that this feels... real, it also feels like the right thing to do.

But I'm not freaking out. I *want* people to know. It'll make it easier for me to cut ties with anyone who gives a shit that I happen to like dudes. I can think of a few guys on the team already who are way too fond of their go-to fag jokes to ever really get it.

Fuck those guys.

I'm bi. I'm fucking my best friend.

And I think I might be in love with him.

"How you feeling?" He asks from beside me.

"Pretty fucking great. You?"

He gives me little shrug, though his smile is so big I can tell he's full of shit. "Y'know. Same as any other day, I guess."

"Asshole," I say with a laugh.

Before he can defend himself, his phone buzzes on the bedside table. He reaches for it and unlocks the screen.

"Shit, it's already almost 8. What time are we supposed to be at the airport?"

"11."

I glance at his screen and see the face of a guy I don't know in his text messages. I can't read what the text says, and I don't want to be the guy who gets all nosy and insecure, but seeing that immediately kills my buzz.

Is he still texting other guys from that app? Still looking for hookups?

Something burns in my gut, and I realize what it is almost immediately: Jealousy. It's fucking stupid, because Derek and I didn't really talk about being exclusive. We didn't talk about any of this. It just sort of happened.

So maybe I was wrong. Maybe this is another hookup for him. Maybe I'm just another hookup. A straight guy he managed to turn. Fuck, I don't want to think that, but now that it's in there, I can't get it out.

I need to clear my head before I make a

complete ass of myself.

Swinging my feet over the edge of the bed, I grab my underwear and pull them on, then dig my sweats out of my traveling bag.

"I'm gonna try and get in a quick run before we leave," I say, trying to keep my voice as even as possible.

Derek is messing with his phone, and at first he doesn't respond. I'm already lacing up by sneakers by the time he answers. "Shit, sorry. You want company? I've gotta make a quick call, but I can meet you out there?"

"Nah, it's cool."

My head is spinning as I let myself out into the hall. I need to get over this shit. Just be a man and ask him what we're doing. But I'm afraid of his answer, and that's what has me hitting the sidewalks outside our hotel right as the sun starts to come up.

CHAPTER TWENTY-TWO
- Derek -

Of all the things I expected Grace to text me, asking for advice about how to sneak back into the house after being gone all night is definitely not on the list.

I almost want to just call Mom and Dad and bust her ass before she gets the chance to try and cover it up. It's not like she's going to get far. She's 16, and there's no way they haven't noticed she's been gone.

I'm pissed at her, because I know she's probably seeing the guy she told me about the last time I went home. My move has been tough on her. But she doesn't need to send our parents to an early grave worrying over what kind of shit she's getting herself into.

I can think up all the threats I want, but I know I'm going to talk her through it. She's my sister, and it's not like I don't have at least a little experience with the subject. I managed to regain Mom and Dad's trust after sneaking out and hitch-hiking almost two hours away to the closest gay bar, so I can probably help her smooth things over.

She's not going to like it, but oh well.

I give her a call and she picks up right away. Just as I guessed, she isn't looking for a way to come clean and apologize, she's looking for a way to somehow get away with it. But she's crying, so I go easy on her I'm 99% sure our parents already know she's gone.

I calm her down and we talk for a bit before

she puts Mom on the same call and tells her what happened while I listen. To her credit, Mom doesn't freak out, and the whole thing's resolved in less than an hour.

I guess my family has become really good at dealing with crises both big and small.

With the phone resting in my hands, I can't help but feel the distance. I try not to let myself get homesick all that often. My grandma is great and the guys on the team feel like a family to me most of the time. But it's hard not to think about the way my life could have gone.

I was being recruited by the Longhorns before my injury, and I would've signed with them without giving it a second thought. I could've come home on the weekends, and then maybe Grace wouldn't be acting out and Mom wouldn't be so worried about me and Dad could stop stressing over how I'm supposed to pay for out-of-state college.

But instead I had to get injured; had to let myself get played by somebody I thought I could trust. Somebody I thought I loved.

Shit. I still need to tell Jason about Danny. I just don't want him to pity me or change the way he acts around me.

Then again, the way he left this morning was already a little weird. I thought we were good. Better than good. But he isn't back yet, and it didn't really seem like he wanted me to go with him when he left.

Maybe I'm wrong about us. Maybe he's having second thoughts.

It's a little after 9 when he gets back, and I'm already showered and dressed. Coach is going to want us down in the lobby soon, and it won't be long before we have to head back to the airport and go home.

But I'm not focused on any of that. Instead, I try to get a read on Jason as he pulls off his sweaty clothes.

"How was the run?"

"Pretty good." He tugs off his pants, balling them up and tossing them onto the bed. "Think I have time for a shower?"

"Yeah, sure."

I'm such a fucking pushover. I just sit there while the water runs and try to think about what the fuck I want to say to him when he gets out. Thankfully he takes showers quick, just like me and every other football player in the world, and when he comes out I can smell the slight scent of soap and hotel shampoo as he walks by.

I reach for his arm and he immediately tenses, then looks at me like everything's going the way it always has.

The last thing I want to do is turn this into some huge drama fest, so I take a minute to not just say the first thing that wants to fly out of my mouth.

"Look, dude, you're gonna have to tell me why you're giving me the cold shoulder if you want me to do something about it."

"Just trying to get ready before the team leaves without us," he says, pulling out of my grasp and going to put on fresh clothes.

I let my hand fall onto my knee and watch him, wondering what the hell happened in so short a time. "Yeah, I can tell it's not just that."

He grabs hanging clothes from the closet, pulling on his slacks and belting them. We're required to wear nice shit when we come back from an away game; especially when we win. It's a team morale and presentation thing, and Jason's always looked damn good in a suit. But this time I can't really get that excited about it.

"It's cool, Griff. We can talk about it later."

That's the first time he's called me Griff in a while; at least when it's just been the two of us. Now I know something's up, and I walk over to him, putting my hands on his shoulders and standing there so he can't just ignore me.

"I wanna talk about it now." After a beat, I try to prompt him. "If you're having second thoughts or something—"

"I saw your phone," he says simply, as if that's supposed to answer all my questions.

I stare at him, bewildered. "My phone? You mean the text from my sister?"

Why would he be pissed about that? Grace isn't his responsibility.

"The one before it."

It takes me a minute to even realize what he's talking about. I only remember reading my sister's text. But then I see a flash of a douchey, smiling face in my mind. Another guy from Grindr who messaged me right after the first and hasn't stopped messaging me since. To his credit, he only does it every few days. Usually to update me on how horny he is. Each time I tell myself I'm going to block him, then I wander off and do something else.

"What, the Grindr douchebag?"

"Like I said, it's cool. Just let me know when you've got hookups planned so I don't drop by your dorm or something."

The Jason I see right now is the Jason who takes the field every Saturday. Cool, collected, and totally unreadable. The guy everybody else just knows as "Hawk."

And I don't like it one bit.

"I don't have any hookups planned, J. The last time I even met a guy was when we went out to Dazzle."

"It's cool," he says again, like saying it more firmly is going to make me believe he means it. "Neither of us ever said anything about being exclusive."

Ouch. Okay, time to put this shit to rest.

"That guy?" I gesture back toward my phone where it rests on the nightstand. "He's just somebody I'm too lazy to block. Christ, Jason, the only reason I opened up my profile was because I was trying not to think about how much I wanted you."

That gets his attention, but I can see him fight it. His blue eyes search mine and I wonder if he's been lied to in the past. He never talks about any of his exes, the same way I never talk about mine.

"So there isn't anyone else?"

The guarded hope in his voice kills me, and I lift both my hands to his cheeks. "There's nobody else. I only ever wanted you." It's too much, and I feel like I've just said something that's going to leave me wide open, so I couch it in humor. "Come on, man. You're my best friend, and I got a hard-on when you tackled me. I thought you wouldn't want anything to do with me if I couldn't figure shit out."

"That would've sucked for you if I was straight," he says, and a small glimmer of a smile quirks at the corner of his lips.

"Yeah, well. Next time wear an ID badge or something. 'It's cool, you can think about me while you're jacking off.'"

That actually makes him laugh and I smile, feeling a sense of relief wash over me. I hate misunderstandings. And while I'm not a guy who pours his feelings out on the regular, I also hate not being able to just talk things through.

I hope what I've said is enough to reassure him. I'm not sure I want to say anything else yet. It's terrible, because I feel it. I feel it every time I look at him. But I just... need time.

So instead, I let my actions speak for me, and softly press my lips to his. It's slow at first, but the longer we keep it up and the closer I press my body to his, the more heated it gets until we're locked in another make-out session that seems like it's heading for the bed.

I don't hear the door open until it's too late.

"Whoa, guess you guys are... busy," I hear Mills say.

Shit. Did Jason forget to close the door all the way when he came in?

Fuck. We have way bigger problems than that. I pull away from Jason and my face is flushed as I meet Mills' gaze. He looks away from me immediately, and starts toward the door again, mumbling an apology.

There's no way to explain this one. Mills saw us going at it, and now it's only a matter of time before the whole team knows.

"Uh, Hawk, hit me up when you're not... busy, okay?"

"Mills, wait." I stop him before he can leave, and close the door all the way so nobody else can drop in on us.

"It's cool, man." Jesus, if I hear that phrase one more time today... "I'm cool with it. None of my business what you guys do anyway."

"That'll teach you to knock next time," Jason says, and his tone is weirdly... teasing.

Mills gives a nervous laugh. "No shit."

"Hey, you mind keeping this between us for now?"

Mills starts to respond, and I can tell he's going to agree no problem before Jason speaks up.

"Why? I don't care if the guys know. Most of them won't give a shit, and anybody who does can fuck off."

A part of me is really glad for Jason's attitude toward all of this. It's nice to be with a guy who isn't a complete closet case and doesn't want to chance being seen together in the presence of strangers, let alone friends or classmates.

But another part of me—a part of me I hate—is freaking out.

Football players aren't always the most open-minded guys. I know that from experience. When my last team found out about me...

"I'd just rather wait."

Jason stares at me; through me. "Wait for what?"

"I gotta finish getting my shit together, so... Later." Mills practically leaves a cloud of dust behind, and I don't really blame him.

That's about what I want to do with this conversation, too.

"Wait for what?" Jason asks again.

"Until..." *Until I know if this is for real.* "Until the season's over. Less chance for drama then."

"What about my dad? Can he know? Or your parents? Have you told *anybody* about us?"

I don't like the way he's looking at me right now. Like I just went back on what I told him. Like I'm kicking him to the curb and he can't trust anything that comes out of my mouth anymore.

I also don't like my answer, because while a part of me wants to tell the world, what actually comes out is: "Not yet, but I..."

The words come out. Jason waits, and I can tell he's getting frustrated, but I just can't do it.

"Whatever it is, you can tell me," he says, taking a step closer to me.

I want to tell him. I want to just come out

with it right now and put all this behind us. But the rational part of me is chained down. Held back by the ugliness inside; the fear I just can't seem to shake, no matter how hard I try.

What if Jason turns out to be just like Danny?

Even as I think it, I know there's no way that will ever happen. Jason's nothing like Danny.

Except for the fact that this might not be as real to him as it is to me. We've never talked about the longterm. I've been too chickenshit to even bring it up.

And I still can't manage it now.

"We haven't—"

I start to tell him we haven't talked about this yet, but the words get stuck in my throat.

I want this thing between us to last. I want to know he's lying beside me when I go to sleep at night, and that he'll be there when I wake up. I want to be the one to make him laugh. I want to tease out that special smile he only gives to me. I want to be his shoulder when he needs it, and help him to back to his feet when he loses sight of what really matters.

I think I might be in love with him.

But if he doesn't know me well enough to realize what a big deal this is for me, what are the chances he feels the same?

"Tell me the truth: Are you ashamed of me? Ashamed of us?"

"You know I'm not."

"Then why make such a big deal out of this?"

198

Something comes over me in that moment. It's like a wounded animal. Defensive and distrustful and cynical as hell, and up until now, it's a part of me that's only managed to take hold when I'm having a really bad week.

But right now, it busts free, and all hell breaks loose.

"Because it *is* a big deal. You weren't the one paralyzed because someone hates what you are, so fuck off, Jason."

As soon as the words leave my mouth, I regret them. I see the surprise in Jason's eyes, and then the flash of pain, and it kills me. I want to apologize. Tell him what a fucking idiot I am. But that other version of me still has a strangle hold, and I just stand there, helpless to fight against it.

"Yeah. No problem," he says, and stuffs his blazer and everything else into his bag, hefting it over his shoulder and walking right past me.

"Jason..."

"Turn in the keys when you leave."

The door closes behind him and I'm left alone, hating myself more than I ever have in my life.

CHAPTER TWENTY-THREE
- Jason -

It's really fucking hard to avoid someone you're forced to see for hours every day.

The first few days are the worst, when I keep wanting to call him or text him to invite him over. For the last couple of semesters, my dorm hasn't been lonely thanks to him. Now every hour I'm alone is something I physically feel as the clock slowly ticks by.

I also never noticed how much my schedule eased up. With Derek, my life wasn't just football. I started focusing on school and other things that are important to me, like family and friends. I'm even getting A's in classes I would've gotten C's or D's in before.

But without him, I go right back to what I know. Pushing myself above and beyond at practice. Hitting the gym for hours on end. Working with my dad on the weekends.

Anything to keep from thinking about Derek.

And the whole time, there's a part of me that wants to pick up the phone; a part of me that thinks I'm being petty. I totally get the fact that Derek's not really over what happened to him in high school. I probably wouldn't be over it, either.

Late Thursday night, I found myself close to caving. I hit the gym instead, and was in the middle of another upper body circuit when my phone buzzed. Expecting just another text, I ignored it until I saw it was a missed call. When the voicemail icon popped up, I couldn't help myself.

Standing in the middle of the gym, I listened to a slurred message from Derek:

Don't delete this, okay? I know I fucked up. I just... I can't... I don't know how to do this. I'm sorry. I'm damaged goods, man. You deserve somebody better than me. Just don't hate me, all right? I don't wanna lose you as a friend, too.

When I lowered the phone from my ear, I realized he'd already given up. On us. On me.

And that hurt even more than what he said.

It's like he doesn't trust me at all. He doesn't trust me to keep him safe, and I get the feeling he thinks whatever I feel for him is just me being bored or something.

Maybe I haven't sorted out my feelings yet, but I know I'm not bored or confused or anything like that, so fuck him for putting that shit on me.

I know I can't think about it right now, so I do what my dad taught me to do when my mom died: I ignore the pain and find ways to keep myself busy and exhausted so it doesn't have a chance to catch up to me.

For those few days, I succeed, mostly thanks to the fact that we're gearing up for a game that's going to decide where we end up playing in the post-season. If we win, we'll be the #1 seed in the SEC, lock down the best record in the school's history, and have a shot at being chosen as one of the top four teams to compete for the national championship.

We're still going to end up at a bowl game if

we don't, but I want the title. Even if it's not officially recognized by the NCAA, it gives me another good mark for the NFL recruiters to look at.

And right now, it gives me a reason to focus and not worry about my personal life.

When game day rolls around, I'm focused. I have to be, because if I let myself think about Derek as anything more than a teammate, I'm going to blow it.

We're playing Alabama, and from the very first drive, their defense makes my life a living hell.

They put the pressure on hard, and there's a point where one of their guys vaults over my offensive line to try and get to me. I have to dump the ball quick, and I throw an easy interception that gets run back for a touchdown.

It's all downhill from there.

I don't know how it unravels so fast, but it feels like pieces of the ground are crumbling out from under my feet, one by one. A fumble here. A blocked field goal attempt there. Countless third downs that don't convert.

By the third quarter, we've only put up 7 points, and we had to scrape and claw for that touchdown. Meanwhile, Alabama has 21 over us.

But I don't completely lose my cool until I see Derek start getting some of the heat I've been seeing all game. I throw him a deep pass like the one that won us the game against Raleigh Tech, and I see him give it his all, trying to shake the two guys who are right on his ass.

Reynolds tries to block for him, but he's outpaced, and by the time Derek gets the ball in his hands, he's completely fucked.

I can hear the hit all the way down the field as helmets and pads connect. It jars through by bones, slicing an ache through my heart that has me practically gasping for air. I have to tear my helmet off just to feel like I can breathe, and I fight for every single breath until I see Derek peel himself off the field and come back to the line of scrimmage uninjured.

"You all right?" I ask as the clock continues to run.

"Yeah. Got the wind knocked out of me."

He takes his place and I get ready for the snap, but my head isn't on the play. Instead, I'm worrying about what would happen if Derek ends up in the same situation again. Injured, and this time because of me. Because I threw him a pass he shouldn't have gone for.

I second-guess myself and hold onto the ball too long. Long enough for a huge linebacker to break through my offensive line and come barreling toward me.

I see him out of the corner of my eye, but by that point it's too late. I can't dodge him; can't hope to run with the ball now. And I'm not ready to take the sack.

When he hits me, he hits hard. I feel something tear, and then the ground rushes up to meet my head. The last thing I see is the blurry sight of cleats before everything fades to black.

CHAPTER TWENTY-FOUR
- Derek -

When the whistle blows, everything moves in slow motion.

I don't know what happened to the ball. I was covered for the whole play, and the last thing I saw was Hawk still holding onto it, like he was waiting for me or Matthews to get open.

There's a crowd of guys back at the line of scrimmage, and all I can think is that he must have taken a sack. My heart leaps into my throat as I jog back. It's only ten yards, but it's the longest ten yards of my life.

When I see the medics rushing out, I realize Jason isn't one of the guys standing around. Time seems to slow to a crawl. Every step is like moving through quicksand.

When I finally shove my way through the crowd, it all stops.

The sounds of the stadium fade away to nothingness. My breath and my heartbeat both seem to seize. I can see the medics moving their lips, but I don't hear anything from them, either.

Jason is laying on the ground. And he's not moving. He's not responding to the paramedics, and for a moment, I can't even tell if he's breathing.

"Jason?"

I don't bother to disguise the panic in my voice. Instead I tug off my helmet and just drop it, pushing and shoving until I can get through to Jason's side.

"Step back, son. Let them do their job." I don't know when Coach Garvey even got here, but he holds his hand out to stop me. As I watch the medics shine a light in Jason's eyes, I can't breathe.

I feel so completely helpless. I just want to scream or cry or demand they let me be by his side, as if that's going to suddenly make him wake up.

When he finally rouses, relief hits me so hard that I almost can't stay on my feet. The paramedics get him onto a stretcher and the crowd roars with applause, but all I can do is try to get in his line of sight—try to catch his gaze to get some idea of whether or not he's okay.

Because he has to be okay.

But his head falls back and he loses consciousness before I can reach him, and Mills keeps me from following the paramedics off the field. As the door to the tunnel beneath the stadium closes, I realize I'm going to have to somehow finish the rest of this game without knowing if Jason is all right.

We lose to Alabama, 42 to 7.

Half the time I don't hear the backup quarterback's play-calls, and I end up missing a couple of easy catches and eventually turning the ball over.

When the assistant coach pulls me from the game, it leaves me in complete agony, because it just gives me a chance to sit there and wonder. I can't leave the stadium. Only Coach Garvey went with Jason to the hospital, and the rest of us have to wait until the game is put out of its misery.

As soon as the final score is called, I go straight to the locker room, drop off my equipment, and grab what I need. A bunch of the other guys do the same thing, and Coach Hanes takes us to the hospital ER.

The waiting room fills up with college football players. I try to reach Coach Garvey on his cell, but he has it turned off. When Coach Hanes goes back to look for him, all I can do is pace.

I nearly jump out of my skin when I feel a hand on my shoulder.

"Sorry, man. Just wanted to see how you're doing," Milla says.

"Fucking fantastic," I say before I can stop myself. After a second I sigh, and try not to be such an asshole the second time around. "Sorry. Just wish they'd tell us something."

"You and me both." He gives me a look that says he knows it's not really the same for us, though. I guess there's an up side to somebody knowing how much I care about Jason. "Holler if you need anything, all right?"

"Yeah. Thanks, man."

I grab a seat because I'm starting to get dirty looks from the hospital's admitting staff. And a few weird looks from my teammates, too. I don't really blame them for wondering what the hell's going on with me. Some of them look a little concerned, but most just look bored. They have their phones out despite the big sign telling them not to. They're making trips to the vending machines or the coffee cart.

They look like teammates. Guys who've ultimately seen all this before and have no reason to think Jason won't be okay.

And no reason to feel guilty.

Fuck. That's the worst part of this. My stomach churns with it, and I just want to shove through those security doors and check every room until I find him so I can apologize for being such a dick.

Maybe I'm wrong. Maybe this wasn't bothering Jason as much as it's bothered me for the past few days. But what if it was? What if he was distracted during the game today? Because what happened out there, it would've never happened to the old Jason Hawkins. He's one of the least sackable quarterbacks in the division, if not the whole damn league.

And it gnaws at me the whole time I'm sitting there. I think about what I could've done differently. How I could've just swallowed my pride and checked all my baggage and just admitted that I was fucking scared. Scared of ending up where Jason is now.

I'm given a good twenty or thirty minutes to agonize over it before I hear the buzzer sound as the heavy doors open outward. Coach Hanes and Coach Garvey both walk into the waiting room, accompanied by a nurse, and I'm the first one on my feet.

"How is he? Is he going to be okay?"

My voice doesn't even sound like me. It's higher-pitched. Panicked.

Coach clears his throat to get the attention of all the other guys who aren't as invested in this as I am. "Jason's awake right now. His dad's in there with him. Doctor says he's sustained a mild concussion, and has a torn ACL."

The word 'concussion' makes my stomach drop. That's one of the worst possible words a football player can hear, because once you get that first one, your chances just get so much worse if you have another. And considering Jason's most likely bound for the NFL, I don't think this will be his last.

And a torn ACL... shit. Our coach back in high school used to tell us that tearing a ligament was way worse than breaking a bone. He made us do stretches and warm-ups regularly to try and avoid it.

But both of those things are secondary in my mind to the fact that Jason is awake. He's alive. Even if I rationally knew he wouldn't be dead, it was hard to quiet my mind after seeing his lifeless body carted off the field.

"I need to see him," I say, standing in Coach Garvey's way before he can take a seat.

"Mr. Hawkins needs his rest," the nurse says firmly. "I'm afraid it's family only right now. If you boys want to come back tomorrow, we can admit a few of you at a time."

"No, you don't understand. I need to talk to him."

I'm never the kind of guy who gets agitated

by people who are just doing their jobs. They have enough shit to deal with as it is. But right now, this nurse is standing between me and Jason, and there's no way I can wait until tomorrow to see him. That's just not going to happen.

I try to move past her, to go for the button that opens the doors, but Coach Garvey stops me.

"Why don't you take a seat, son. I'm going to have the bus come by and get you all back to your dorms."

"I'm not going anywhere. I need to see Jason."

"Derek, it's okay. He's okay." There's a warning in Mills' voice, and I know exactly what it means.

If I disrespect my coach and act out here, there's a good chance I might not start in the next game. But I don't fucking care. I don't care if I never start in another game. If I never get that scholarship. If I never get my degree.

I just need to make things right with Jason.

"I'm going back there."

I shrug out of Coach Garvey's grasp and hit the button. The door slowly opens again.

"I'm sorry, sir, but unless you're family—"

"I'm his boyfriend."

The words come out before I even realize I'm saying them. I can hear dead silence in the waiting room, and when I look at the nurse, she glances to Coach Garvey and Coach Hanes before addressing me.

"I can let you back for a short visit, but once the doctor comes, you'll have to leave."

I don't try to fight it anymore. All I need is a chance, and I follow her back through the ER, barely hearing the low din of my teammates.

The ER looks pretty slow, and I'm grateful for that. If I went back there to find Jason was being parked in the hallway, I would've been pissed. Instead, he's in one of the bays, behind a curtain. It's not much better, but at least it's something.

When I step past the curtain, the first thing I see is Jason's dad in the nearby seat. He has his reading glasses on and a book in his lap. Anger flares in me. Why the fuck isn't he right by Jason, talking to him or trying to make him more comfortable? Who can read when their kid is hurt?

But when I actually look at his face, I see lines I swear weren't there the last time I saw him. Maybe he's just really good at keeping all of this shit inside. Right now, I could probably use a lesson or two from him.

He's not why I came here, though, and when my gaze settles on Jason, I feel even worse. He's in a hospital gown now, instead of his uniform. There's a band around his wrist and he's got an IV hooked up to his arm, along with a few intimidating monitors.

He's paler than he should be, and when he looks at me, he looks... hopeless.

"Hey," I say lamely.

"Hey."

I swallow hard and come over to his bedside. No way am I going to make such a big deal about coming back here and not actually man up enough to talk to him. Moving my hand over the gurney railing, I reach for his hand and entwine my fingers with his.

I can feel him tense at first, but he slowly relaxes. His dad is watching us, and I find myself not caring whether he suspects or not. Jason wanted everybody to know. Now they do. For better or worse.

"Do you mind if I talk to him for a bit?" I ask, my heart already hammering in my chest.

"That's fine. You want anything from the machines, Jason?"

"I'm good, thanks."

His voice sounds bleak. Colorless, if that's even possible. Once Jason's dad draws back the curtain and I hear him retreat down the hallway, I take in Jason's appearance more fully. Despite the things I noticed earlier, he's intact. He just looks like someone told him he only has a few hours left to live.

And even thinking that makes my stomach roll.

"I'm really glad you're okay," I say, and I don't really try to hide the emotion in my voice.

"Yeah. Sure. Except for the fact that I'm out for the season."

Right. The ACL tear. That's going to need surgery and a long, difficult recovery. Losing that mobility is just suicide for a quarterback.

It's sad that a part of me is glad for it. A very tiny part, but one that still exists. If he isn't on the field, he can't get hurt again.

But looking at his face, I know he's already

in pain. And not just the physical kind.

"Your dad will get you the best physical therapist out there. Maybe there's still a chance you can get well enough to play before January."

He shakes his head. "Doctor doesn't think so, and Coach was in here when he said it. I'm done, Derek. I'm not going to the bowl game, and I might as well forget about the NFL."

"Hey, don't talk like that. You can still go to one of the camps. Nobody's going to turn you away once you're healed. So what if you aren't drafted?"

Even I know it's a long shot. The NFL doesn't have to make up the majority of their teams from walk-ons. They can be a hell of a lot choosier than the universities. But I refuse to believe Jason doesn't have a shot. He's an amazing quarterback. Anybody who watches his footage will see that.

"You should've seen my dad's face when the doctor told me I wouldn't be playing for the rest of the season," he says, and I can hear the change in his voice.

Out of everything he's said to me so far, that's what's causing him the most pain. I want to go out into the hall and tell his dad he should be fucking grateful that's the worst thing that happened to his son.

Instead, I force out the words: "He's just worried about you."

Jason doesn't say anything, just looks up at the TV above my head. It's muted, and when I glance over my shoulder I don't see any closed captioning, so I know he's just trying to avoid my gaze.

"Jason..."

I take a deep breath. I've needed to say this for days. I hate that it's taken something like this to get the words out of me, but I can't hold them back now. The last thing that matters here is how scared I am for myself. Whatever happens, I'll deal with it.

I just want Jason and I to be okay.

"I'm sorry for what I said in your dorm. It was fucking stupid and selfish and I wasn't thinking straight."

"It's fine," he says, shifting in his bed.

"No, it's not. I was a real dick. You're the first guy I've been with who's ever been cool with going public, and I just... I acted like an asshole. I let what happened in the past get inside my head, and I fucked everything up."

He looks up at me, and I can see the hesitation in his eyes. "You did act like an asshole."

"I'll make it up to you, I promise."

"Yeah? You're going to be the one getting me water and shit while I'm laid up in bed?"

"Fucking right I am. I'll put in the transfer to your dorm myself."

He shakes his head, but a little smile makes its way to his lips. At least he doesn't hate me. And when I take his hand and gives his fingers a gentle squeeze, he doesn't try to pull away, so that has to be a good sign.

"There's something I want to tell you," I say, putting my other hand over top of his. "About

216

what happened to me in high school."

Jason looks up at me cautiously, but slowly nods.

I draw in a deep breath. Every part of me wants to turn back. There's a reason I don't let myself think about this shit. But if I want this thing to continue with Jason, I have to tell him. He has to know why I'm so fucked up. Why I made a big deal out of it.

"I told you the guys on the team found out I was gay, and that's why they didn't block for me." He nods. "Well, they found out from one of my teammates. A guy I was dating. Danny." I take a second to figure out how I want to say this, and pull up those memories I haven't touched in years. "Danny was the first guy from school I dated. The others were hookups. Older guys who didn't know I was underage. Other kids at a gay bar. But Danny was somebody I actually cared about, and I thought he cared about me. Around six months into it, though, the other guys on the team started to give us a lot of shit about always hanging out together. Called us fags. Made sure we could hear whenever they made gay jokes. I guess Danny freaked out, because he started pulling away. Wanted to see me less and less. Eventually, he said he wanted to break up. I was pretty fucking crushed, but I focused on football and tried not to let it bother me. Next thing I know, everybody on the team knows I'm gay, and every time they say something about it, there's Danny at his locker with his mouth shut, looking guilty as fuck."

I wish I could say I'm not angry about it,

but even now, it hits me hard. My jaw clenches, and I have to stroke Jason's hand to calm myself down.

"When I was laid up at home, he came over to visit. Wanted to clear his conscience, I guess. Told me he was the reason the guys knew about it. That they wouldn't leave him alone, so he gave me up instead."

"Jesus," Jason says, and there's a roughness to his voice that tells me he's affected by it, too.

"Needless to say, I haven't talked to the guy in years," I say with a smile I don't really feel.

"That's really fucked up."

"Yeah."

We sit quietly for a few moments, and I'm a little relieved Jason doesn't make a huge deal out of it. I can tell it pisses him off. There's tension in his body that wasn't there before. But I can also tell he's thinking about something, and I let him get it out, turning my attention to the silent TV for a minute.

"You know I'm not going to do that, right?"

"I know," I say, turning back to him. "You've been great about this. I'm the one who's been stupid."

He shrugs a little. "I'd probably do the same thing."

I don't really know what to say. I don't deserve someone like Jason Hawkins. The fact that he not only seems to forgive me, but gets why I acted the way I did is mind-blowing to me.

"I guess I was afraid that if the guys found out, it might happen again. But this place is a lot different from the town I grew up in."

"Less rodeos?"

It's so out of the blue that I have to laugh. "Yeah. Less rodeos. Asshole." My smile fades as I remember what I said in the waiting room, though. "Anyway, they all know now, so I guess we'll see what happens."

Jason's brow furrows. "What do you mean?"

"I told them you were my boyfriend. In the waiting room. They wouldn't let me back here to see you."

"Shit, D," he says, and I try to decipher if he's just a little awestruck, or angry.

Even now, it's hard for me to believe that a guy like Jason Hawkins—good-looking, popular, a celebrated athlete—would be totally okay with everyone knowing he's seeing a guy.

"And here I thought *I* didn't do anything half-assed," he says with a little smile.

I've never felt more relieved in my life.

"You're okay with it?"

"I told you I was."

I just nod. It's still a little surreal, but my heart lifts. It's almost like the last two weeks never happened. Like the last few hours never happened, too, even though I'm standing here at Jason's hospital bed.

"Are you?"

I should've expected the question, but it still catches me a little off-guard. I have to take a minute to think about it; to make sure I'm giving him the most truthful answer. Even if I already know what I want to say.

"Yeah, I am. Not gonna lie—I'm still fucking terrified. But whatever. We'll figure it out. I don't want to go through the last couple weeks again, Jason. You mean too much to me."

The surprise in his eyes makes me realize just how much I've said, but the slow smile that follows makes me not care.

"Me, too."

I smile right back at him, then bring our joined hands up to my lips and kiss his fingers.

My mood simmers a bit as I hear the sound of his dad's boots coming closer. I can even feel Jason tense against me.

"Think he knows?"

He just nods. "Yeah. I don't exactly make a habit of holding hands with a lot of guys, Derek."

I smile, but a fresh rush of anxiety fills me. I know how much his dad's opinion means to him. He may not care what the world thinks of us being together, but there's a good chance it would hurt him deeply if his dad turns out to be anything less than supportive.

Patting his hand, I reluctantly let go of him, jerking my head toward the curtain to let him know what I'm planning to do. As I head out there, I don't have the words in my mind. As I come face-to-face with James Hawkins, I have to grasp for something to say.

"How is he?" He asks, and his voice is as haggard as I've ever heard it.

Maybe it will be okay. It looks like he genuinely does care about his son, and not just the fact that his son is a football star. I guess we'll find out one way or the other.

"As good as he can be, I guess." His dad nods slowly, and I take a second to screw up my courage and say what needs to be said. "He's having kind of a rough time with this. Maybe you should go easy on him?"

He studies me for a moment, and I can see the response that wants to form on his lips. His jaw is rigid, and I'm just waiting for him to snap down and bite my head off. But the brusque side of him I've seen with Jason never comes out. He just sighs and runs a hand through his graying hair the way I've seen Jason do a million times.

"Yeah. I will."

"I'm gonna wait out here in case he needs anything." At least until I'm chased off by the doctor. "Just let me know."

It kills me to leave Jason's side, but I have to trust his dad to do the right thing.

CHAPTER TWENTY-FIVE
- Jason -

I don't have enough time to figure out what I'm going to say to my dad before he comes back into the room.

From the time I woke up and found him at my bedside with Coach Garvey, my stomach has been in one big knot.

It's weird. I always thought that if I got injured, I would feel it personally. Not just physically, but mentally and emotionally, too. And I do, but not for the reasons I would've guessed.

The idea of not being able to finish out the rest of the season sucks. Knowing that I may not be able to make the NFL after everything I've done throughout my entire life is even worse.

But this whole time, I've just been thinking about how my dad is going to react to all of it. He's the one who put in the time. He's the one who put in crazy hours at two jobs to support us both.

Sometimes, it feels like he has more riding on this than I do. And I just don't know what he's going to think of me when I tell him it may be all over.

But I have to say something. There's no way I can go through the long process of recovery without knowing what he thinks one way or the other.

Derek's given me the strength to confront my dad, and when he enters the hospital bay alone, a cup of coffee in his hand, I don't feel as much anxiety as I thought I would.

"Derek's just outside," he says, as if he can sense the fact that I'd rather have my friend—my boyfriend—here.

"It's cool. I want to talk to you anyway."

He nods, and does that thing with his jaw that he always does when he's trying to steel his own courage. The last time I saw him make that face was at mom's funeral. That really doesn't bode well for me.

Before I can say anything, he takes a seat at my bedside, looks down at his hands, then starts to say what's on his mind.

"Listen, Jason. We never talked about any of this. I wish I could say I saw it coming, but I guess I had you so busy with football that you never really had time to figure it out. I just want you to know that I'm... Okay with it."

It takes so much effort for him to choke that out, but I don't want to assume. I have to ask what he means.

"Okay with what?"

"With you being... The way you are. Gay. Or... Whatever you want me to call it."

I swallow hard. It's difficult seeing a man I've respected all of my life have such a hard time talking to me. Then again, the relationship he and I have has never been the talking sort. The very fact that he can get this out is... Touching.

And I'm not going to correct him. I know it's probably a big deal for him to accept this as-is. I don't want to complicate things by telling him I'm bi, or give him some false hope that I'm just going through some kind of phase or something.

"Thanks, Dad. That means a lot."

He nods slowly. "Derek is a good boy. A good man."

I smile. "Yeah, he is."

"You've changed since he's been around. I think... I think he's been good for you."

I do, too. But I never expected my dad to agree. Maybe there's hope for us after all.

I let the conversation lapse into silence, until all I can hear is the slow beeping of the pulsox monitor. I try to think of how to phrase it—how to best break it to him—but I can only find one way.

"What happens if I can't finish out the season?"

He was here when the doctor told me it would be highly unlikely for me to play in the bowl game. If that's true, it means this is the end of my college career, either way. The NCAA won't allow me to play any games next year, even though I'm slowly facing the fact that I'm going to need another year of school just to graduate.

"Never say never, Jason. You've worked your ass off for this. The doctor's just talking about people who sit around all day and don't put in the time."

"But what if he isn't? What if he's talking about the best case, and it's going to take me a year or more to get better?"

"Don't say that," he says quickly, and there's such pain in his voice that it kills me.

Pain, but not anger. Maybe he's accepting the fact that my dreams are going to have to

225

change, too.

"But what if it's true? You know the NFL isn't going to want me if I'm injured."

"Then I'll take you to every tryout in the goddamn country until we find one that sticks. As soon as you're better, we'll hit them all. I'll my job, we'll sell the car, I'll just —"

"Stop," I say, and it comes out as more of a plea than a command. I just can't hear him talk like this. "I don't want you to sell the car or quit your job. I don't even know if..."

I can't say the words. It's too much. Everything we've worked for is unraveling in one fell swoop.

"You don't even know if what, Jason?"

I let out what has to be the deepest breath of my life. "I don't even know if I want to play in the NFL."

He doesn't say anything. His jaw clenches, and I can tell he's holding back. I suddenly wonder if Derek got to him.

Either way, I decide to take advantage of the fact that he's letting me talk.

"Football is all I am, Dad. It's all I've been since middle school. This past year, I finally had a chance to live a life outside of it, and... I like finding out who I am." He still doesn't say anything, and I sigh. "Don't you think there's more to me than just football?"

"Of course I do. I wouldn't have pushed you so hard if I didn't think so."

"I love playing football. I love everything you've done for me, and all the time we spent together because of it. And I really hope..." I choke on the words, clearing my throat. "I really hope that doesn't change if I decide not to play professionally."

The look that passes across his face is one I can't decipher. It seems pained, but in a different way than before. It's as if he's finally coming to terms with something, and I have no idea if his reaction will be good or bad.

"It won't change anything, Jason." He swallows, then clears his own throat. Like father, like son. "I love you. No matter what. And I'll support you no matter what. If you want to give professional ball a try, I'll do everything in my power to make you ready for it. If you decide you want to be a doctor or a lawyer or something, I'll stay all up all night with you studying for whatever the hell tests you have to take."

I laugh, even as I feel a hint of moisture prick at the corner of my eyes. "Yeah, let's not go crazy."

He gives me the most genuine smile I've seen from him in years. "Good. I don't like lawyers. Or doctors."

He reaches for my shoulder and gives it an affectionate squeeze. I clasp my hand over top of his for a moment and smile. It feels like a huge weight has been lifted off my chest.

"Well. Now that that's out of the way, you want me to call Derek back in here?"

"Sure. I've got something to say to him, anyway."

I have a lot of things to say to him, actually.

But only one of them I'm going to say in front of my dad.

He ducks around the curtain, and I hear him call for Derek. They both enter, and I see my dad looking at him in a different way. A little wary, sure. But it seems like he's as proud of Derek as he is of me.

Even laid up in a hospital bed like this, with my future completely uncertain, it feels amazing. That's something I would've never been able to say last year.

And I know it's all because of Derek.

I swallow back the sudden swell of emotion as I look at him. Gentle brown eyes look back at me, and his soft lips draw into a slow smile.

"Everything okay?"

"Yeah," I say. "Better than okay."

He glances at my IV bag. "That's the painkillers talking."

I laugh, even though it hurts. I think I may have bruised a rib hitting the ground so hard, too. But it doesn't matter. None of this does. I can see that now.

"I'm not contagious, asshole. Get over here so I can tell you something."

He arches a brow, then looks at my dad, and I know exactly what he's thinking. When he comes over to my bedside, I reach up for the collar of his shirt like I'm on my deathbed and I'm giving him my very last request.

"You better win that fucking bowl game, or I'm breaking up with you."

He just laughs, his relief obvious. "Yeah.

I'm on it."

DECEMBER

CHAPTER TWENTY-SIX
- Derek -

The weeks leading up to the Outback Bowl have been a blur for me.

I skipped all the holiday stuff with my family because I wanted to spend time with Jason. That of course meant actually *telling* them about Jason, and while both of my parents were supportive, my mom now texts me every other day telling me how much she can't wait to meet her 'future son-in-law.'

Christ.

So that's going to be a thing when the season's through. I'm not really nervous about my family meeting Jason, because I think they'll love him. But I am nervous about him meeting them. He might decide it's a little bit too much; that he doesn't really want to do the whole domestic thing.

He's been doing really well with recovery so far. Despite loosening his grip on football, he still comes to every therapy session with a crazy amount of intensity. I attend as many as I can with him, and help him exercise his knee under the therapist's guidance.

It's slow-going right now, because he's still coming off of the surgery. He's basically having to work on strengthening exercises and limiting the potential for injury.

Seeing the therapist work with him every day, and watching Jason go from frustration to confidence has honestly been pretty inspiring. The NFL has never really been on my radar—not since high school—but I've also never really decided what the hell I wanted to do with my life.

Until now.

True, I have a bowl game to get through, not to mention another year of school. I'll probably end up busting my ass as a senior, just trying to get in the right classes to prepare for it. But I really want to work in PT.

Even if the scholarship doesn't happen next year, I'm determined.

For now, though, I have a promise to keep.

The team bus took us to Tampa for the bowl game, and we're facing off against Michigan. They're ranked #5 in the country and, like us, they weren't one of the teams invited to compete in the post-season tournament.

They're favored to win by every major paper and network, but the guys are all planning for an upset.

As I suit up in Tigers blue and black for the last time this season, I feel like I've come a long way from that first practice jersey. Even getting on the field again was a struggle for me, and I wouldn't be here if it wasn't for Jason. He's a born coach, and I really hope he'll consider it once we're out of school.

Mostly, though, I'm feeling proud of myself

because I haven't freaked out yet about the fact that all of my teammates know about Jason and I. Yeah, I've probably lost some potential friends. Not like I'd want to hang out with those guys anyway, though, and I can deal with the fact that it sometimes gets quiet in the locker room when I walk by, or that Matthews has made a habit of learning more gay jokes so he can be sure to say them in front of me.

Whatever. As long as I still have Jason, that's all I need.

Of course, I never anticipated getting actual notice outside of my teammates, and when a reporter barges into the locker room before the game, I'm as shocked as everybody else.

She easily gets lost in the sea of guys and lockers. They give a few predictable wolf whistles, but I hear Davies tell them to knock it the fuck off. As she looks around the locker room, I assume she's trying to get an early scoop—a read on how morale is doing before the game, and what we're planning as far as strategy is concerned.

She's not going to get it. Coach has made sure we don't breathe a word of it. I haven't even been able to tell Jason.

But when the reporter's eyes meet mine, I see recognition there. She pulls out her phone and comes right up to me like we're best buds.

"Are you Derek Griffin?"

"That's me," I say, watching as she pulls up some kind of app.

The guys beside me stop what they're doing, all in various states of undress. She doesn't seem to care, and I'm guessing if she's willing to duck inside the guy's locker room before a big game, this isn't her first rodeo.

"Sasha Everly, Orlando Sentinel. I'd like to ask you a few questions, if you don't mind?"

I glance toward the coach's office. Coach Garvey is in there with Coach Hanes and Coach Gonzales. None of them are paying attention to the locker room right now. If they were, security would definitely be on its way.

"You can ask. I can't guarantee an answer."

I expect her to ask about my stats or our plays or what I think of Michigan's defense. Typical stuff.

But that's definitely not what comes out of her mouth.

"How does it feel to be a gay player in Division-1 football?"

I just blink, half-gaping at her. She's asking me about being gay? I look around to see if maybe the other guys are pranking me, but they look just as stunned.

"I..."

"Do you ever feel judged by your teammates, Mr. Griffin? Would you say football is an accepting sport?"

I don't know what to say to any of that. I almost feel like I should have a lawyer present, or at least somebody who handles Eastshore's PR. I look toward the coach's office for help again, but they're still busy.

"Great," I hear Matthews say from a row over before he rounds the lockers. "Instead of focusing on the game, now every paper's gonna call us 'the team with the fag.'"

"Shut the fuck up, man," Mills says.

"Is this the kind of reception you normally get?" She asks me.

"No, it isn't," Carter says. "Nobody here gives a shit. Griff is a good player, and whatever he chooses to do off the field is his business."

"Speak for yourself, cocksucker," Matthews continues.

I've never wanted to punch that asshole more than I do right now. Unfortunately, Mills beats me to it. 300 pounds of solid muscle channel into his fist and connect with Matthews' face. He's knocked off his feet and stumbles hard against the lockers.

Then he lunges for Mills.

That finally catches Coach Garvey's attention, and he, Hanes, Gonzales, and a couple security guards break up a fight that now involves six different guys. Nobody notices the reporter until the dust clears, but soon after she's escorted out of the locker room.

Holy shit. This was the last thing I wanted. And as I run out of the tunnel with the other guys less than a half hour later, it has me rattled.

But as soon as my number is called, the stadium just erupts in applause. I'm so inside my own head I don't notice it at first, until West nudges me with his elbow and points up to the crowd.

It looks normal at first. Lots of signs. Foam fingers. Streamers. The sort of thing you would normally see at a bowl game, in both teams' colors. But dotting the packed rows of people I see rainbow signs. Rainbow body paint. Rainbow everything.

From down here, it's hard to make out what they say. When I look up at the screens, though, they're focused on one sign in particular, and I can clearly read it:

We support Derek Griffin

The camera pans across a few others. *Football is For Fags*, written in a way that I'm guessing isn't the same as how Matthews would mean it. *Eastshore Diversity Club Supports Derek Griffin. I Came Out Because Of You. You're My Hero. My Dads Love You, Too.*

Jesus. By the time they start focusing on the field instead of the crowd, I've practically got tears in my eyes.

I never wanted to be this guy, but if this is the positive side? Maybe it's worth all the negatives.

With the crowd on my side, I play my fucking heart out.

It's just the sort of thing I needed, since Jason isn't here. His therapist didn't think it was a good idea, and for once, Jason decided to not be stubborn. Mostly I think it was because of his dad's suggestion that they could kick back with a few beers and watch the game together. So even though he isn't here, I know he's seeing every second of it.

I wonder how he's reacting to the fact that the stadium roars every time I get a completion.

I know I feel fucking fantastic about it. I've never let the crowd get into my head before, but this time I think it's helping me, and our whole team. Even though Michigan comes out with a strong start, scoring a TD that doesn't go answered until the second quarter, we're playing the best football we've ever played.

By the time we reach the half, we're still trailing by 7, but we've managed to put 14 points on the board. One of those was from my run-in, and I thought I was going to go deaf from how loud that crowd was when the play was made.

Coach Garvey gets us fired up with one hell of a pep talk in the locker room, and there's not a guy on the team who isn't prepared to give it all they've got. Even Matthews has shut his fucking mouth for once and is focused on the game, finally working with me instead of against me.

The back-up QB, Taylor, is no Hawk, but he gets the ball down the field consistently and puts plenty of pressure on Michigan. Most of the third quarter crawls by with both defenses getting the job done, until the last two minutes when Taylor makes an amazing drive.

We're set back by a penalty, though, and it becomes first and goal on the 20 yard line. The pressure's on, and there's no way he's going to be able to run the ball in. Our running back is stopped both times, way short of the goal line, and we come up to it at third and 13.

Taylor calls for the audible and I switch places with Matthews in the backfield. I run toward the goal, but there's a Michigan guy right on my ass, apparently managing to guess exactly when the ref's back is turned. He grabs my jersey and even my mask once, and I try to shove him away, but he's too strong.

On the other side of the field, Matthews is just as fucked.

Taylor is looking for someone to throw the ball to, and when I see it fly toward me, I wish to God he would've chosen Matthews, or just chucked it to a tight end. There's no way Michigan isn't going to pick it off, and the best I can hope for now is a touchback.

I do what I can, and out of the corner of my eye I watch one of the linemen sprint faster than I've ever seen before. The guy covering me doesn't see it coming. He's taken down and I can hear the wind get knocked out of him. It's such a fucking shock that I almost don't catch the ball.

Almost.

I leap for it, jumping over the tangle of players, then pivot to the side. I run it in, and it seems like everyone's on their feet in the stands.

This could've so easily been a repeat of high school. My heart thuds in my chest as I jog off to the sidelines, my teammates patting me on the back. They were there for me. Throughout this whole game, they've been there for me. To them, I wasn't 'the gay football player.'

I was just another guy working his ass off, determined to win.

In the end, it came down to a field goal late in the fourth quarter. We pulled ahead by 3, and got it to stick as the clock ran out. Final score: Eastshore 24, Michigan 21.

I knew everyone would call it luck, but most of us played career games. We were the best we've ever been, and when I was handed the MVP trophy, I truly believed I'd deserved it. All of the blood, sweat, and tears had been worth it.

But I knew I wouldn't be here without one specific person.

So, standing up there at the podium, with cameras flashing in my eyes, I tell the world the truth.

"I'd like to thank the players and coaches who worked with me this season to help me get where I am today. But I want to dedicate this award to the real MVP: Jason Hawkins. Hawk couldn't be here with us tonight. I know he's watching this at home, and probably yelling at his TV right now," I say with a grin, already knowing it's only going to get worse.

I'm riding high on a mix of adrenaline and euphoria, and I'm fucking giddy. Raising the trophy up, I look straight into the nearest camera.

"You gave this team your all, so this trophy belongs to you. I love you, J." After a beat, I add, "And there's no take-backs on national TV, so deal with it."

CHAPTER TWENTY-SEVEN
- Jason -

I can't believe he said that. On national fucking TV.

Holy. Shit.

Derek Griffin loves me.

It doesn't matter how I run it through my head, I can't get over it. I just sit there, staring at the TV, all these emotions rolling through me at once. Trampling over every thought, every sense, everything I am.

It takes me the entire commercial break to realize I'm not just watching this at my dorm where I'm completely alone. I'm watching it at my dad's place, and he's sitting right here in his recliner while I'm on the couch.

He saw the game. He cheered and swore right along with me. Yelled at the refs for bogus calls. Lost his shit when drives were stopped just short of a first down.

And he saw my boyfriend confess his love for me in front of an audience of journalists and sportscasters.

I glance over at him, and he's already looking at me. I wonder how long he's been that way, just cautiously watching my reaction. Maybe he's waiting for me to look happy or mad or something inbetween.

Right now, I'm still in shock.

"Hell of a way to accept an MVP award," he says simply.

I could almost laugh because it's so

ridiculous.

Derek was freaking out about the team knowing. Then he just up and told everyone I was his boyfriend. Now he's a gay superstar to the crowd packed into that stadium, and he's gone and one upped himself yet again.

When all of that sinks in, I can feel a slow smile spread across my lips. It takes its time, eventually tugging into a grin that starts to make my cheeks hurt.

Holy shit. Derek loves me. And I love him. I have to tell him. I have to do *something*.

I reach for my phone before common sense catches up with me. Even if he's in the locker room now and has it on, there's no way he'll be able to hear me during the celebration.

And really, I don't want to do this over the phone.

But I'm not going to see Derek until Monday, at the earliest. And that's being generous, because he and the rest of the guys will be swarmed by the whole town. I can't imagine getting alone time with him until sometime later in the week.

I'm not really sure I can wait that long.

"Dad... do you need me for the weekend?" I ask even before the plan fully forms in my mind.

He doesn't answer for a long moment, and when I look at him, I can see the worry in his eyes. Not disapproval, which is what I expected. Just worry.

"Are you going to leave anyway if I say yes?"

"Probably."

A small smile touches his lips. "Okay then. But you're not leaving until after dawn tomorrow, and you're going to take it easy once you get down there. If I hear you re-injured yourself, you, me, and Derek are gonna spend all spring at the gym. Got it?"

I love you too, Dad, I think, but instead I just say: "Got it."

I wasn't able to fall asleep until late into the night. Too much nervous energy and excitement. Exhaustion finally took hold around three, and I got up just after seven, setting my alarm for the crack of dawn.

After a quick shower and breakfast I was on the road and headed for Tampa, a four hour drives.

From about nine onward, my phone rings and buzzes every half hour or so. I glance over the first time and see Derek's picture, and it's so hard not to answer him and tell him what's up.

But I want it to be a surprise, so I drive my old Accord with the radio cranked up, and I try to plan out what I'm going to do and say, but I never really come up with anything concrete.

Of course, once I get into town and punch the hotel's address into the GPS, I realize there's a really good chance Derek and the team won't even be there. They've probably got press conferences and other shit to go to today before they head back home.

But fuck it. If that's the case, I'll wait. Turns out it was a good attitude to have, because I end up having to do just that when the concierge tells me the team is out for the day.

Thankfully he recognizes me from my picture on TV, so he helps me get upstairs. He even winks at me as he hands over a keycard to Derek's room, and I feel my face heat up like I'm sixteen again and being caught sneaking in through the window.

I guess I'm doing the same thing here. When I slide the keycard into the door, my heart's already racing, even though I know he won't be there.

His room's pretty neat, all things considered. It looks like some of the guys came over last night and had a mini-celebration. There are beer bottles sitting out on the table, and some pizza boxes in the trash.

Derek's bed is unmade, so he probably slept in until they were all called out to go do whatever it is they're doing right now. The concierge said something about a big lunch with the owner of the Bucs.

As much as I wish I could be by his side, I have no interest in crashing that party. For one, it probably requires a suit and tie, and all I brought was one change of clothes and a fuckload of condoms.

For another, as soon as the guys see me they'll be all over me. And as happy as I am for my team, it's really Derek I want to see.

As I sit down on his bed and wait, I realize

that I have no idea whether or not he's rooming with anybody. Fortunately when I check the closet I only see his luggage, and I count my blessings. It's not often we get our own rooms, but I guess fate's on my side today.

The cleaning lady drops in around noon, and I scoop the bottles into the trash while she chastises me for helping. But frankly, it gives me something to do.

I'm about to go crazy just sitting here.

It's about two in the afternoon when I finally hear familiar voices in the hall. My heart pounds hard against my ribcage, and my breath catches in my throat as I wait to hear the beep of Derek's keycard.

When he finally turns the heavy handle, I'm standing in the middle of the room, trying not to feel more nervous than I already am.

Derek pulls the door closed behind him, not seeing me yet. He has his phone in his hand, and he's texting someone. When my phone buzzes in my pocket I can't help but smile.

Derek's head snaps up, and he almost drops his phone. "Holy shit."

Because I can't help it, I lift up my own phone and text him back a 'hey.'

"Holy shit!" He repeats, walking toward me cautiously, like I'm a mirage or something. "I've been texting you all day. I thought you were fucking pissed at me, man."

"I didn't want to answer you on the phone," I say, and I wonder if his heart is beating as wildly as mine is when he walks toward me.

He stops in front of me, and we take each other in for a moment. I can see the happiness in Derek's eyes, but I know he's waiting for me to acknowledge that I heard him during that MVP speech.

"First of all," I say, "you'd better keep that fucking trophy."

He laughs nervously, reaching out to touch me. It's tentative at first, again like he's checking to make sure I'm really here. He just runs his hand up and down my arm.

"And second..."

I draw in a deep breath. I haven't had a lot of practice at this. Any practice, really. I hope I can manage to say the right shit.

"You're my best friend, D. For a while you were the only one who saw me as anything but a football player. I love you for that."

His smile is bright and infectious. I can see his dimples, and even just the slightest hint of moisture in his brown eyes. He laughs again, and the happiness in that sound squeezes around my heart.

Before I know it, his hands are on either side of my face and he's pulling me in for a kiss.

It's slow and sensual and a confirmation of everything that's happened between us over the past season. When it breaks naturally, he's wearing a little smirk, and there's mischief in his half-lidded eyes.

"Just for that?"

"No, not just for that." One of my hands rests against his neck, and I stroke the pad of my thumb over his stubbled jawline. "I love the way you always end up kneeing me in the back while I'm trying to sleep."

He groans. "We really need to get a bigger bed."

"I also love the way you bite your lip a little when you smile at me."

"I do not."

He does. He's doing it right now, and I can't resist moving in to kiss him, my own teeth nipping lightly at his bottom lip.

"I also love the sounds you make when you fuck me," I say, my voice lowering.

I feel him shudder against me, and he holds back a completely different groan. Desire lights in his eyes, but he bites his lip again.

"What if I don't fuck you?"

"You better. I drove all the way from Tampa."

He grins, moving his hands down to my ass and bringing me fully against him so I can feel him through his pants. He's already getting hard for me.

"Good point. But... I'd let you fuck me first, if you want."

A twinge of desire hits me at the offer. "Yeah?"

"Yeah. As long as you take it easy," he says, capturing my lips again. "And since you did drive all the way from Tampa..."

He slowly slinks down my body, his knees hitting the carpeted floor. He unzips my fly, looking up at me the whole time. His eyes are still half-lidded with desire, but there's something else in his expression that I didn't really allow myself to notice before: Real affection. Love.

My heart clenches in my chest again, but I'm not given much time to enjoy the more subtle feelings as he tugs down my pants and underwear. My cock is already almost fully hard, and when it bobs free, he wraps his hand around the base, giving me a few good tugs.

He doesn't waste any time, and I watch as his lips slide over the tip. My head falls back and I let out a moan, not caring who hears me. He works me slowly, not just exploring like we did the first few times, but expertly knowing exactly what to do to get my rock hard and ready for him.

When I start to feel my balls tighten, I let out a shuddering gasp and curl my fingers into his hair, pulling him up. I kiss him, hard, and start moving him back toward the edge of the bed, pushing down on his shoulders firmly so he sits on it.

I start to drop to my knees to return the favor, but Derek stops me. Right. My knee. I've got full range of motion now, but it's probably not a good idea to push it. I don't need to end up in my doctor's office trying to explain how I re-injured myself.

Derek scoots back on the bed and motions for me to join him, tugging down his pants and boxers. I lean over him, my hand gripping around his cock. I savor the taste and the feeling of him in my mouth, the groans and moans and grunts that I draw from him with every flick of my tongue. The more noise he makes, the more my body starts to ache, until all I want is to bury myself inside of him and give him the same kind of pleasure he's given me.

After paying a lot of extra attention to the head of his cock and bringing him to the point where he's almost whimpering for more, I pull my mouth from him and look up at his face. His whole expression is changed by desire. His cheeks and neck are flushed, his long lashes flutter over his closed eyes, and his lips are parted in pleasure, just begging to be kissed again.

I can't resist. My tongue presses past his lips and I explore his mouth, teasing and tasting him.

"Lay back," he says, breathless when I finally break the kiss.

I scoot back on the bed, kicking off my shoes and tugging off my shirt. He does the same, giving me the chance to admire his body. I still want to trace every line, every dip, every swell of muscle with my tongue, but right now I need to feel connected to him in the most intimate way possible.

He climbs overtop of me, his knees on either side of my thighs, and he pins my hands to the bed by the wrists. I claim his lips again, and slowly roll my hips to grind against him, skin to skin. His moans practically vibrate through my whole body, and they're soon joined by mine, until I can't tell which sound belongs to him, and which belongs to me.

"Jesus, D, you're killing me," I say, my voice rough and strained.

"Tell me what you want."

He rolls his hips against me, his dick rubbing over mine. I squirm beneath him, trying to break free of his grasp. I know I could probably do it if I really wanted to. He's not holding on that hard. But I think he likes this little game, and it's definitely turning me on.

"Want you to fuck me. Please."

Even if either of us had any interest in drawing this out right now, I can tell there's no way he'd be able to resist a plea like that. Letting go of me just long enough to grab my bag, he fishes out a bottle of lube and a packet of condoms, getting us both ready.

He straddles my hips, and my heart's pounding wildly. I don't want to hurt him, or do something he won't enjoy, but seeing the trust in his eyes makes me feel like it'll all work out.

He lowers himself slowly, tensing at first before he slowly relaxes. I can't help but hold my breath, trying to keep myself from moving too much inside of him.

He doesn't stop until his thighs are flush against mine. I feel him clench around me, and I can't hold in the moan anymore. It tears from my throat as I let myself experience what it's like to be inside of him; to be connected to him completely.

I've never felt anything more amazing.

CHAPTER TWENTY-EIGHT
- Derek -

Jason Hawkins is going to be the death of me.

I told him when we first started this that I've bottomed before, but it hasn't been often, and it's usually a lot harder for me to get off that way. The tops I was with never seemed to have a clue what they were doing, and they always just pushed and shoved until they got what they wanted, maybe remembering to reach around and jack me off if they were feeling especially generous.

But it's different with Jason.

I know he's never done this before—not with a guy, anyway—but he's taking so much care with me that I have plenty of time to adjust to his size. He's bigger than I thought, nice and thick, and when I get him a few inches deep, he presses right against that spot that makes my whole body suddenly freeze, a slave to the intense hit of pleasure.

I grip the edges of the bed, and lift my ass up to give him a better angle to penetrate me. When he lifts his hips and his big cock sinks into me fully, I let out a loud, low moan.

It's an unreal sensation. A feeling of fullness and an awareness of his every movement, from the slightest twitch to the very moment I start to ride him. When his hips push upward again, he hits that same spot, and I arch against him, wanting him deeper inside of me.

Fuck. If I knew bottoming could've felt this

good, I would've done a lot more of it. But as great as it feels, I know it's because of my partner. Being fucked by Jason is an experience I can't even describe, and when I can manage to pry my eyes open long enough to meet his, it's just beyond amazing.

We move slow and steady at first, then, as I relax even more and the lube works its magic, he starts to pump into me, meeting me halfway each time, and I've never seen anything sexier. Watching his muscles flex as he fucks me, seeing the expressions he makes and the way he's totally losing his composure is the best thing I can ever imagine.

I can feel him hit deep, satisfying something inside of me I never even knew I wanted. But it's the more shallow movements that have me moaning and panting and begging, to the point where I have no idea what I'm saying. I'm his completely right now. His to bring over the edge, and when he does it, I can hear my own shout bounce off the hotel walls.

White hot pleasure streaks through me. My hands grip the edge of the bed hard, but I can't feel any pain from it. The sensation of ecstasy is too strong, and it's ramped up even more when Jason thrusts into me one last time before he comes.

When I force my eyes open again to watch him, I can tell he's experiencing the same sort of bliss I am. His face is contorted in pleasure, his lips parted, a deep moan pulling from him. I can still feel him inside of me, and it makes the whole experience that much better; that much more intimate.

We're both left panting, almost gasping for breath. I keep him inside of me, not wanting to let him go yet, and both of my hands thread into his hair as we kiss.

I can't think of a more perfect way to end this season than being here, wrapped up with the man I love.

MAY
16 Months Later

CHAPTER TWENTY-NINE
- Jason -

It took Derek and I forever to save up the money to move into an apartment, and that was with some advanced graduation money from our families.

Derek took a tutoring job and I did some private coaching for high school kids looking to be recruited. The result was a two bedroom apartment that probably costs more than it's worth, honestly, but it's ours. Derek and I were both grinning ear to ear when we signed the lease.

We moved our shit in after the semester ended, with some help from Mills and a few of the other guys. Now it's set up with a bedroom, a little "home gym" that's really just some space for exercise mats and kettle bells right now, a living room where we've got an old TV and his Xbox, and a bathroom and kitchen. There's a little back porch area, too, and Mills bought us a charcoal grill as an early housewarming present before he had to start getting his ass in gear for the NFL draft.

Now it's furnished, mostly with Craigslist finds and a couple pieces from the IKEA in Jacksonville. Neither of us are that picky, but D's already warned me his mom will probably have a fit.

They're coming today. His whole immediate family. Mom, dad, and sister. Everyone's in town for the graduation ceremony, and I'm already nervous as hell about meeting them.

"Dude, you look like you're about to pass out. Stop freaking on me," he says, putting a hand on my shoulder.

"Fuck you, I have to meet three people who'll give me shit today."

There's nothing even a little bit hateful behind my words, and Derek knows it. I'm glad to be meeting his family. Nervous, yeah, but glad. And Derek's spent the past couple weeks assuring me they're going to love me. Apparently I'm all his mom asks about when she calls.

"Nobody's going to give you shit," he says, and that familiar glint of mischief lights in his eyes. "Unless you start telling people that we've already broken in every room of this place."

I groan at the memory. That was one of the first things we did, after agreeing it would be "good luck." Once the furniture was brought in, we decided to try for "good luck" a handful more times, just to be safe.

What can I say? We're both pretty shameless. And there are days when I can't be alone with him for more than a few minutes before I want to get my hands on him. I know he feels the same about me.

But today, we have to keep it in our pants. At least for a few hours. People are going to start showing up any minute, and as much as I love the hit of adrenaline that comes with cutting it close on time, I don't really want to be caught fucking by Derek's parents. Or my dad.

Our guests start arriving around six. My dad's the first one, since he lives in town. He drops by right after work, and Derek sets him up with a beer on the couch. The three of us talk about the upcoming draft and who we think is going to be picked by which team. Mills is probably going to the Panthers, which isn't too bad of a drive from here, so we make a plan to drop in on a couple games if he starts.

Our mutual friends trickle in after that. Mostly guys from football, but we've got a few gay friends now. Derek met Christian after the Outback Bowl, when the team came back to town. He and his boyfriend Blake have been pretty cool, and we usually end up doing the kind of double-dating I can get behind: Hanging at the Tigers' Den, watching a game and knocking back a pitcher of beer.

About an hour later, Derek gets a call from his family saying they've just now hit the tarmac. Apparently the scattering of rain we've had today delayed their flight, and he heads off to the airport to pick them up.

By the time he gets back, I've had a couple beers and feel a lot more mellow than I did earlier, but my heart is still pounding hard as I hear voices out in the hall. When the door opens, I expect to see Derek leading the group. Instead, a petite, middle-aged woman looks at me with wide eyes.

"There he is!"

Before I can even think to respond, she closes the distance between us and wraps me up in a pretty impressive bear hug for such a small woman. I think she's probably crushing about ten different bones in my body.

She pulls back, lifting her hands to my cheeks. "You're so tall!" She looks around, sees some of the other guys. "Oh sweet Jesus. You are Jason, aren't you?"

Derek laughs from behind her. "Yeah, Mom. That's Jason. Good to know you're just into hugging random guys now, though."

"You hush," she says, and hugs me again. When she pulls back this time, there are tears in her eyes. "It's so good to meet my future son-in-law."

"Evelyn..." A deep voice warns.

Derek's dad is closer to him in height, and I can see the similarities between them. He wears glasses, though, and it's terrible that my first thought is how sexy Derek would look wearing some slick frames.

"It's good to meet you, too, Mrs. Griffin."

She smacks me lightly on the chest, and I look at Derek in surprise. I can tell he's about one second away from just completely losing it.

"Don't you dare call me that, young man. It's Evelyn. And this is my husband Robert."

I extend a hand, and Derek's dad meets it in

a firm shake.

"Heard a lot about you," he says. "Hell of a player."

My dad stands, and I introduce him to the two of them. It's worth it to see how awkward he looks when Mrs. Griffin—Evelyn—hugs him, too.

There's only one person missing...

"So you're the guy who's boning my brother."

Standing next to Derek is a teenage girl who's packing serious attitude into what has to be less than a 5'5" frame. Blue streaks in her hair, ripped jeans, and a t-shirt featuring a band I've never heard of pretty much complete the package exactly as Derek described.

"Thank you for that, Grace," Robert says in a voice that I can tell means 'we'll talk about this later.'

"She's just jealous of me," Derek says, slinging an arm around her shoulders.

She rolls her eyes but doesn't shrug him off, and I can't help but smile.

Once introductions are made, Derek's mom orders him back down to the car to bring in groceries, and I expect maybe a bottle of champagne or some finger food until we can get the grill fired up. But no, she bought enough groceries to cater for the entire graduating class, and she takes over the kitchen like a whirlwind.

"Best to just stay out of her way," Derek warns me. "She can get pretty vicious with a spatula."

"I heard that," she says, and I feel Derek

cringe next to me. "Honey, this kitchen is pathetic. We're going to Kohl's first thing in the morning to get you some more pots and pans."

Derek just shrugs, and I laugh, shaking my head. He was right. His family's already treating me like a son. His dad has even taken up residence on the couch near mine, and they're watching SportsCenter together over a couple beers. Grace, meanwhile, examines the contents of our fridge. She pulls out a beer, but it's quickly intercepted by her mother.

"So Derek tells us you're planning to become a coach after you graduate, Jason? What level?" Evelyn asks.

"High school," I say, and Derek threads his hand with mine, giving it a squeeze to let me know he's proud of me. "And actually... I already have a job offer. The high school a couple miles from here needs an offensive coach."

"That's wonderful news!"

I can't help but smile. It's fucking amazing news, and I only just heard about it this morning, so I'm still riding out the high from it. I honestly didn't expect to get a paid job right off the bat, but Coach Garvey put in a good word for me, citing my experience working with Derek, and then the up-and-coming QBs I helped over the past year, even though I wasn't part of the team.

It's not the NFL, but... I'm okay with that. Actually, I'm great with it. Playing football is awesome, but nurturing a love for the game in someone else? I think I'm really going to enjoy my job.

"And Derek, honey, did you ever hear back from that... What was his name? Finch?"

"Yeah, Tom Finch. I'm going to shadow him for a while, then work as his assistant."

I return the squeeze Derek gave me earlier. After everything he's been through, it still amazes me that he just always keeps going after what he wants. And for him, it's not a career as a professional athlete, either. He's officially finished up all of his preliminary classes, and now he just has to do his internship and pass the state test to become licensed as a physical therapist.

"I'm so proud of my boys," his mom says.

It's only a few words—probably something she didn't even have to think twice about. But her eagerness to just invite me into her family fills me with a warmth I didn't know I was missing in my life.

Sitting in our new apartment, surrounded by friends and family, I've never felt happier. And it's all because of Derek.

He took me from Hawk the "star quarterback" to Jason, a guy who's recognized for more than his ability to throw a football. And even though we haven't officially talked about it yet, I'd like to spend the rest of my life thanking him for that.

THE END

Made in the USA
San Bernardino, CA
17 March 2016